THE WARDEN'S SON

C. G. COOPER

"THE WARDEN'S SON"

By C. G. Cooper

A portion of all profits from the sale of my novels goes to fund OPERATION C4, our nonprofit initiative serving young military officers. For more information visit OperationC4.com.

Want to stay in the loop?
Sign Up at cg-cooper.com to be the FIRST to learn about new releases.
Plus get newsletter only bonus content for FREE.

DEDICATIONS

JC, thanks for telling me your story. I hope this fictional tale puts an exclamation point on your childhood :)

Paul L., your talent never ends.

Glenda, you inspire me with your heart and dedication.

And a big thanks to our Beta Readers: Marry, Paul, Michael, Melissa, Sue, Sandy, Connie, Nancy, Cheryl, Don, Larry, Julie, Dawn, Gayle, Donald, Bob, Judith and Bernie.

PROLOGUE

I guess the most important thing to say upfront was that the summer of 1987 was a pivotal time in my life. I was ten. I made a new best friend. And I became a murderer. Yep. You heard right.

The summer of 1987 was the ninth stop for yours truly on the great prison tour of my childhood. Every year a new town and a new prison to explore.

I wasn't yet a murderer. Not at the beginning. Just the plain old son of a warden wearing jeans with permanent grass stains and threadbare sneakers that wore on me more than I wore them.

Now I wear a suit every day, Sunday through Saturday. I guess in the grand scheme of things it's not the worst quirk to have. I'm not addicted to pills or buying dishes on late-night TV. No, I'm that guy who, in the world of going more casual, has decided to wear a suit. Sometimes I'll even wear a vest to really take things up a notch. My wife calls it my chauffeur look.

I got the suit thing from the warden. That's Dad. It was his thing first. We still talk from time to time.

Life as the son of a federal prison warden never felt weird until I turned ten. I was still a naive waif until that nasty summer when everything changed.

Now I sit here in my suit, so far removed from the boy of 1987 Virginia that I feel like I'm perfectly qualified to judge him. But when the window's open, all I have to do is touch a breeze that carries the gluey stink of split black locust, or hear the froggy grind of a woodcock's call, and then I'm no longer qualified. There I am, back under the hot sun, at the edge of the creek stinking of heat and moss. I am that boy again. And I can make out the line of Redcoats marching in ramrod-straight formation along a pink-feathered sea of mountain laurel in the distance . . .

CHAPTER ONE

The jolt of the car hitting a pothole shook me from ice cream dreams.

I moaned through a yawn.

Dad had the driver's side window cracked and blew a long line of smoke through it.

"Another hour," he said. He had a pretty good grasp of child-speak.

I knew better than to answer this with a further complaint. The warden preached patience.

"Only a little while longer, Jimmy," Mom said, not looking up from the book she was reading.

I looked over at Larry, who was sucking his thumb, his blanket plastered to the side of his face. He was half asleep, so I did what any big brother would do.

I nudged him in the ribs and said, "Sucking your thumb is for babies."

"I'm not a baby!" Larry barked, fully awake now.

"James Michael Allen," the warden said in between

cigarette pulls. His voice was gravel tough, honed from decades of leading some of the toughest men in the federal penal system.

"Sorry, Dad," I said, and threw a stuck-out tongue at my brother. He responded with a shit-eating grin—one point, Larry. I'd get him back for that later.

"Hey, why don't we play a game?" Mom said, clapping her book shut as if giving up on it forever.

"Mom." I drew her name out like a train horn.

She turned around in her seat. "Jimmy, you used to love road games."

Larry said, "Would You Rather!"

"How 'bout it, Jimmy? Want to play *Would You Rather*?"

I rolled my eyes and wished I'd kept my big mouth shut. Larry plus Would You Rather equaled a miserable game of nonsense. So, I did what any well-behaved son of a prickly prison warden would do and gave my little brother a high-flying middle finger.

"Dad! Jimmy flipped me the bird!"

My dad pulled the station wagon to the side of the road as casually as if he'd planned it. I watched his right hand put the old beast in park. The slow, crotchety tick of the parking brake came next.

Shit, I thought, even though I knew every angel in heaven was cursing me for thinking the word.

After sliding another cigarette from its holster, lighting it and taking a deep drag, Dad turned to face me, curls of smoke seeping from his nose like a sick dragon.

I could bear the occasional spanking or tongue lashing. At that moment, Dad was in no position to spank me, given our schedule. A tongue lashing wasn't part of his usual repertoire. Something much worse was. His *eyes*. Eyes that had faced down inmates, riots, irate prison guards, and politicians alike. If *they* caved under those eyes, I was toast.

"Lie down, James," he said flatly. "I don't want to hear another word out of you until I say it's allowed."

My cowering body assented before my mind could object. I lay down, closed my eyes, and silently cursed myself for being so stupid, thinking words that would make the angels blush.

CHAPTER TWO

S later, Virginia was what I'd become accustomed to in terms of federal prison towns. Small.

"Ice cream!" Larry shouted, pointing out the window.

"Yes, honey," my mom said, taking in our new hometown. "Once we get unpacked."

Stifling my groan was impossible. If there was anything worse than moving, it was unpacking. We had a tradition for unpacking in our family. No, I used the wrong word. Tradition implies something friendly, something that bonds you to a treasured past. Unpacking was personal torture disconnected from everything.

As if being ripped away from yet another set of friends wasn't bad enough, I'd get dragged across the country, plopped into another no-name town, and be expected to unpack my entire life within twenty-four hours. That didn't mean just putting boxes in my room; it meant emptying each one, putting posters on the wall, and each pencil in its place.

"Do we have to unpack today, Mom?" I asked, suddenly grasping on hope. "Maybe the movers will be late." I barely kept the excitement from my voice.

"Don't even say such a thing. You know what happened the last time the movers were late." She motioned with her head to my father, who was fiddling with the radio.

I made an "oops I forgot" look, to which my mom nodded.

The last movers. Sheesh. That had been a real mess. They'd been three days late. That was three days sleeping in a sleeping bag on a concrete floor thanks to a delay in re-carpeting the warden's house.

Well, let me tell you. The last thing you want to do if you're a mover is to keep Warden Allen waiting.

The moving crew arrived looking like extras from a Three Stooges film. The driver, who was the owner of the company, met my father on the walkway leading to the front door.

"The highways were a real bear," he said. "You wouldn't believe the wrecks we passed. Hell, I'm not even gonna make any money on this trip what with all the stops we had to make, the hotel stays, you know how it goes."

If he was looking for sympathy, he should've tried Hall-mark. Maybe if he'd come with a simple apology, my father would've acted differently. Yet, he continued hurtling excuse after excuse, and my dad stood there, puffing away on his second of two packs that day.

Finally, when the guy didn't look like he was going to shut his mouth, Dad raised his right hand. The mover's mouth stopped mid-syllable. I think that's when he realized he was in deep fertilizer.

"Have you been paid for time?" my father asked.

"Well sure, but—"

"Okay. Then you will unload our goods and be on your way."

Oh, only fools would continue to speak after Warden Allen had made a decree. The guy said, "But—"

"Are there any details of your story that I missed?" Dad

said. "Is your grandmother sick? Did your cat die? Did your dog eat your grandmother?"

The man's face scrunched in utter confusion. "No, sir, but—"

Warden Allen's hand went up again. "No more. Just get it done." The warden started walking to the house.

Remember what I said about fools?

"What the hell am I supposed to do about the lost time?"

Dad kept walking, slow, not looking like he cared a bit.

"You'll be hearing from me!" said the fool.

Dad stopped, dropped his cigarette on the walk, and ground it to flat cinders with his toe.

I'm glad I was hiding, because there was a good chance he'd have whooped me good had he known I was there.

"You do a lot of business with prison employees?" he said as he turned and faced the mover.

"It's most of my business," the man confidently said, as if it put him in an untouchable spot. He puffed out his chest like an arrogant peacock.

"Well, sir, you can be sure that this is the very last business you'll ever have to worry about with this organization."

"You don't have that power."

"Don't I?"

Now, Dad did something that he only did when someone really tickled the wrong nerve: he *smiled*.

It was cold and about as far from a kind gesture as the Heimlich maneuver is from a bear hug. This guy was, in a word, toast.

The owner-driver disappeared, yelling something about finding a phone, but he was too late. Dad made his call first. The guy came back Bozo-faced, blubbering apologies, but Dad would hear none of it.

I later heard, through the kitchen vent, that the man had

lost his contract with the Bureau of Prisons, and his company went bust.

Like I said, only fools.

CHAPTER THREE

Only a warden's son would go on to tell you what's great about a prison. I'd rather not break precedent.

For starters, the reservations, the grounds of prisons, were the stuff of my dreams. Prisons are usually quite a way from civilization with fields and streams—in abundance.

The Slater Federal Penitentiary looked like an old fort, all stone, and stretches of barbwire fencing. I was used to the fencing and the towers. When you grow up under their shadow, it's just another minor detail in an otherwise exciting landscape.

I pressed my face against the window as we approached our new home. Stately dogwoods lined the entry drive, and the grounds guard patrol offered a polite nod from his truck as we rolled by.

"What do you think?" Dad said, pointing through the front windshield.

"Oh, it's beautiful," my mom said, her voice genuine. She was an easy read. Her words contained none of the drippy sweetness they had when she was placating us.

"I can't see," I said, trying to stretch my seat belt to get a better view.

Our car rumbled over a slight rise and, I saw it. The sight took my breath.

"A fort," my mouth said, eyes wide.

I heard my mom and dad chuckle. They were waiting for me to notice.

Oh man. This was it. This was *my* house. I would be Rochambeau assisting General Washington, heading up the Yorktown campaign to force the hand of that lousy prig Cornwallis.

Large wood beams made up the exterior of the log home. A single-story, tall. And yet, in my youth, I would've sworn the place was a football field wide with a wrap-around porch lighting the way.

"Oh, Dean," Mom said. "It is beautiful."

She was probably seeing the flowers of every shape and color lining the porch. My ten-year-old brain didn't give a flying fig about flowers. No, my ten-year-old mind was already thinking of the perfect spots for snipers to pick off Cornwallis's advance guard.

"Hurry, Dad," I dared to say.

Maybe it was because of his excitement, but Dad didn't tell me to pipe down. Instead, he said, "There's one more surprise."

I strained harder to see.

"What is it?" I asked.

"Yeah, what is it?" Larry parroted. I hated when he did that.

"You'll see. It's next to the house," Dad said.

I focused on where he was pointing. Damn my shortness. Dad took pity on me. For the first and last time, he said, "Take off your seatbelt, James."

It was off like a dead man's noose. I stood with a hand on both front seats.

I saw a mini log cabin, a replica of the big one, right where Dad had pointed.

"Is that my room?" I exclaimed, nearly short of breath, hoping beyond hope that that was my surprise. Mine, not Larry's. My *own* house, without that pain in my ass sneaking in and taking my toys. It was like going to college.

Dad laughed. Mom giggled.

"It's not your room," Dad said, "It's your *fort*. The inmates used it as a model before they built the big house. They never tore it down. Thought you might like it."

I was the type of kid who shook a birthday card after removing the fifty-dollar bill that came in it. It should come as no surprise to anyone that I was a little miffed that I didn't have an apartment of my own at ten. Thankfully, that disappointment subsided quickly. Hell, this was a dream. Maybe Mom and Dad would let me camp out there. Oh, the war plans I would hatch from that mighty redoubt.

"Hurry up, Dad!" I said, not caring about a punishment. None came. Dad was enjoying the show as much as I'd ever seen him enjoy, well, anything.

We skidded to a halt, and I was out the door faster than spilled mercury. The mini-cabin, which I immediately dubbed 'Fort Wilderness,' was perfect. It even had a heavy-hinged front door to keep marauding Indians (not to mention those treacherous redcoats) out.

I eased the door open, not wanting to spoil the sanctity of the place. Inside was better than out. I didn't care about the dirt floor. And who the hell cared about the smell of old earth, like when you turn up the ground after a thaw? All I cared about was the tiny window, perfect for sniping and for spotting the enemy before they attacked.

This one room was bigger than any bedroom I'd ever had.

There was plenty of space for rations for the winter, extra ammunition, and weapons. I could fit at least thirty—no, *fifty* of my closest colonial friends who'd left their farms to pillaging forces and suited up in the name of freedom.

My imagination swirled from planning battles to fighting in them. Then Larry ran in.

"Yay!" he said, nearly knocking me over as he bull-charged into my place.

"You can't come in here."

He ignored me, doing a funny little hop to try to grab one of the windows and heave himself up.

"Help," he whined, wanting a boost. I could've toppled him right the hell out of the window altogether.

"No, you little weasel. This is *my* fort."

Bad move, Jimmy.

Larry turned and puffed out his chest. I knew what was coming next.

"*Mooooooommmmmm!* Jimmy said I can't play in the fort."

And then, to my dismay, my utter horror, a stake in my ten-year-old heart, I heard the dreaded words.

"James, the fort is for you *and* your brother."

The freedom fighters were screwed. There was a redcoat in our midst.

CHAPTER FOUR

Move-in day was every bit of dreaded disgust I knew it would be. When I wasn't checking off the carefully-numbered boxes as the movers carried them in, I was unpacking them. Dishes. Frames. Gardening tools. Clothes.

On and on it went. All the while, I tried to steal glances at my fort. Larry was out there now, soiling the place with his presence. Mom had given him a box of toys and told him to stay in the fort. Great. An indomitable colonial redoubt littered with GoBots.

I, on the other hand, had to work, and I wasn't even getting paid!

Still, I knew better than to complain. I consoled myself by thinking about the many summer days I was going to spend in my new Shangri-La. Maybe I'd dress Larry up as a French general and burn him at the stake for treason.

"Hey, kid. Before I have to shave again," murmured one of the movers who was looking down at me as he was sweating huge drops.

"Sorry," I said, snapping from my daydream. "One sixty-nine," I read off the box. Then I crossed off the number from the list on my lap.

The mover grunted and went on his way.

Mom glided in with a tray filled with tall glasses of iced tea.

"Can I have one?" I asked, my mouth salivating. It was summer in Virginia. That meant *hot*. Even hotter since my dad wouldn't let us turn on the air conditioning until the movers were gone. No sense wasting money, he said. The warden was always careful not to spend a penny of federal money on anything he considered extravagant. Apparently, not dying of heat-stroke was a luxury.

"It's a privilege to be employed here," he'd say to us, to the guards who had to be nudged back in line, as well as to politicians who came to visit. The warden repeated it—like even he needed to believe it.

So, no AC and no iced tea.

"They're for the movers," Mom said, patting me on my sweaty head as she moved past. The old lady would probably make me pass up cookies she served at my funeral.

I noticed there wasn't a ring of sweat anywhere on her body. How did she do that? Not only that, she was decked out in one of those baby blue summer dresses like she was going to a company picnic.

I watched her go from one mover to the next, handing each of them a cold, blessed, perfectly sweet drink. I would've openly drooled if I had any saliva left. I cursed under my bone-dry breath.

"James," I heard my dad say, "come to the backyard, please."

At least that took me out of my clipboard duty for a moment. That buoyed my spirits until I thought that maybe it was a ploy to get me to clean latrines or dig a ditch. Not that my father had ever made me do either adult task, but, as you're about to find out, I had quite the imagination. Maybe scraping bones of dead inmates . . .

Dad was fiddling with a black tarp when I emerged outdoors, shielding my eyes from the raging sun. I imagined Mercury and Venus getting incinerated when the sun suddenly started sucking in the planets, one by one.

Dad said, "I thought it was time you had a man's set of tools."

The old man was always trying to get me to take a liking to tinker with everything from a broken toaster to the prison cars on their last leg. In my mind, broken-down vehicles were for the scrap heap, and busted toasters were for blowing up with firecrackers.

He then moved aside, just enough so I could see what the tarp was hiding. As he yanked the rest of the tarp away, I caught my breath.

"A four-wheeler?" I asked in wonder. Of course, it was. I wasn't blind, but I might be suffering the advanced stages of heat exhaustion and hallucinating.

It was a four-wheeler!

Imagine the British scum I could mow down with this thing. I pictured my long colonial hair streaming in the wind, howling my rebel yell, hot on the heels of my prey.

"It needs a little work. I figured we could get it running together. However, it'll be your responsibility."

Without thinking, I rushed forward and wrapped my arms around my father's waist.

"I promise, Dad. I'll take care of it. I promise."

I didn't get the drop-to-his-knee hug. The planets weren't aligned properly for that. All I got was a pat on the back and a contented grunt.

"So," he said, stepping out of my embrace and brushing a

bit of dust off the four-wheeler, "a real man should have a name for his vehicle. What do you think, James?"

I didn't have to think. I knew. Looking back now, Dad probably wanted me to name it a girl's name.

"Marauder," I said. It was perfect.

Little did I know the trouble I'd get into on that thing.

CHAPTER FIVE

Moving-day ended precisely twenty-four hours after we'd arrived. Larry was the only one who'd gotten a full night's rest. I was haggard but reminded myself that the four-wheeler was waiting. There were so many things to see, so much to explore.

"That's it," Mom said, adjusting the picture of my great-grandfather, the first warden in the Allen family line. He was Dad's hero; he was mine by default.

"Impressive job, team," Dad said, fishing a cigarette out of another fresh pack. He went through his routine of tapping it against the pack, sliding it to the perfect place between his index and middle fingers, and then lighting it. He inhaled and then exhaled, totally unconcerned about the smoke that haloed his children. "We've got company coming for dinner."

I groaned deep inside, a place Dad couldn't see or hear. Another night of putting on the perfect son show.

"I'll need to pick up a few things," Mom said diligently. Caretaker, cook, lead unpacker, conflict resolution expert, and hugger of our family, she rarely complained, and never in front of my dad. "I can take the boys with me if you need to work," she said.

"That's okay. I can keep the boys."

This was new. There was a proper order to the Allen family arrivals:

1. We unpack.
2. Dad goes to work.

If Mom was surprised, she sure as hell didn't show it. "You're sure?"

Dad nodded, blowing a thick stream of smoke up at the ceiling. "I thought we'd go exploring. "

"Yay, exploring!" Larry said, jumping from one foot to another. He had a Barbie doll in one hand, a gift from an old friend at the last prison. Our only friends were girls, daughters of the assistant wardens. Dad had been trying to pry the doll from Larry for weeks. She was naked and stained with mud, and her hair was a ratty disaster. She looked like a blonde Neanderthal.

"Okay. The grocery list is on the table if anyone needs to add anything. I'm leaving in ten minutes."

Mom left to get ready. She never left the house unless she was fully decked-out in what I would come to identify as proper warden wife attire: respectable, makeup, shoes with a heel, the whole nine yards.

"Okay, boys. Train leaves in five minutes. Hit the head and put on your shoes," Dad commanded.

Our initial exploration turned out to be an inspection of the farthest perimeter of the prison. I should've known, but I didn't care. This expedition gave me a chance to recon my new battlegrounds. I noted fallen logs where enemy snipers could take potshots at my troops. I mentally jotted the lanes of approach that I could lure the redcoats into and slaughter them piecemeal.

There was an apple orchard in one section of the reservation, the fruit still ripening in the summer sun. Dad lifted Larry to grab one.

"Don't eat it," Dad said. And it wasn't until that moment that I realized how much joy the idea of Larry suffering a three-hour bout of diarrhea could bring me.

The stone prison walls were always in view as we made our tour. Grass tickled my chin in some places, and fields of clover covered my shoes in others. I'd tear up that clover doing figure eights and donuts with my four-wheeler. In other words, the place was perfect.

When Dad finished his inspection, we headed for home. Larry was dragging by then, so Dad hoisted him up on his shoulders. It was amazing how he could keep my brother up there while he puffed away on cigarette after cigarette. It's like he had a third arm just for smoking. I envied Larry, much like I usually did for his lax life.

The day was blazing, and I realized I should've brought water. Dad didn't think of stuff like that. Mom did. Dad's tack was to tough it out. I'm not sure it ever really dawned on him that Larry was a little kid, and I was ten. I suppose it's hard to understand children when you grow up around men who've never experienced childhood themselves.

"I'm thirsty," Larry said for the eighty-seventh time.

"We'll get some water in a minute," Dad said.

We came upon the set of houses we'd seen from a distance on the way out. There were four of them, painted white and neat as a magazine cover. At the first house, a little boy that I guessed was three was running from one end of the porch to the other, his diaper bouncing.

Someone roared, and the little boy squealed. I almost dove for cover. Maybe it was my imagination coupled with the extreme thirst, but for a second, I thought it was a ptero-dactyl attack.

The tall man hulked out of the front door, arms arched and hanging like a looming monster. The little boy squealed again, but he was laughing, trying to get away.

The blonde man scooped up the kid and played like he was going to tear out the boy's entrails with his teeth. He nibbled away as I watched in wonder. I know now that this was what a real dad does. At the time, it was strange. And this man, this giant in my eyes, was the movie star of prison work-ers. He was good looking, like some surfer I'd seen on the commercials of Saturday morning cartoons between G.I. Joe and He-Man.

The man set the boy on his feet when he saw Dad.

"Afternoon, Boss. Didn't see you there."

Dad walked forward; his hand extended.

The men shook and then looked down at us.

"Hi boys, I'm Denny Bell, assistant warden. This here's Bobby." He tickled the little boy who giggled away, nestling his face in his father's chest.

I liked this man immediately. There was something about the way he'd greeted us. This wasn't some guy kissing the warden's ass by being kind to his sons. This was someone who seemed like he wanted to know us.

I stepped forward; hand extended as Dad had done.

"James Michael Allen," I said. Big important folks always said their full names like that when they wanted to appear significant and essential.

The assistant warden chuckled and shook my hand, firm but not bone-crushing the way Dad liked to do.

"Call me Denny, James. At least, if that's okay with your dad."

He looked at Dad, who nodded.

"You can call me Jimmy."

"Say hi to Bobby."

"Hi Bobby," I said reluctantly. I'd learned well from the ass-kissers. Be nice to the kid when you're trying to get in an adult's good graces.

Bobby was put on the ground when he squirmed. Then the kid did something that disgusted me beyond all measure of telling. He ran over and hugged me, hard.

I braced against it. It was like being hit with a bucket of snot. I felt my face flush as Denny laughed heartily. At least he thought it was funny. Go with it.

"We'll see you at dinner?" Dad asked.

Denny scooped up his child again. "Looking forward to it." He took a sniff of Bobby's rear and made a face. "Phew. Better take this one in for an oil change."

There were no goodbyes. That wasn't Dad's style. He turned and left before I could say goodbye to the man who could quite possibly be the *coolest* adult I'd ever met.

As we made our way back home, my dad exhaled smoke in rhythm with each fifth step, and Larry whined like a rusty gate. All I could think about was how I was going to make an excuse to see my new idol again.

CHAPTER SIX

I'd showered and changed when Dad announced, loud enough for the whole house to hear, "Family meeting." He never had to yell. He had one of those voices that cut through air like a spear—a voice primed by years of getting his job done.

I whipped a comb through my hair, making sure to get a perfect part. I hated having messy hair. It took me enough tries that I heard Dad say, louder this time, "James."

"Coming!" I said, huffing in frustration at the moving target that was my hair part. The Allen hair had to have been part of some gypsy curse some five generations before. Off I went, chucking the comb in the sink and tucking in my button-down shirt.

I was expecting our dinner guests. I was wrong. It was another ceremony I'd completely forgotten about in the excitement of the move-in.

Three prisoners stood in a straight line on the far side of the living room. They wore blue overalls, none looking particularly scared or overly cocky. I'd learned to avoid both types.

The scared or shifty ones were unstable in my experience, and the cocky ones made you *think* they were stable.

"Come here, James." Dad motioned to a spot next to my mother, who was standing with her hands folded in front of her.

I hurried to my appointed spot, taking in our staff, as we called them. These were inmates in good standing who were in charge of taking care of our lawn and various other tasks around the house. Working in the warden's home was supposed to be a good deal for prisoners. Dad always said they'd earned the privilege. I didn't completely understand that at the time, though I do now. Who wouldn't want to be outside the prison walls for the day? There's a reason the poor bastards hang their arms outside the bars.

"Gentlemen, my name is Warden Allen, and this is my family. My wife, Esther."

"Pleased to meet you," she said.

"My youngest son, Larry." Larry waved shyly from behind Mom's dress. "And our newest arrival, my oldest, James."

"You can call me Jimmy," I said, doing my best to imitate the assuredness of Denny Bell.

"Starting with you," Dad said, pointing to the man on the farthest left. "Please tell us your name and your current responsibilities."

This man looked very near one hundred years old to my young eyes. He had more wrinkles than an elephant sucking a lemon tree.

"They call me Harley, Boss. Ma'am. I'm in charge of landscaping for your house and Boss Bell's."

I knew Harley was his last name. All the inmates I'd ever met either had gone by their last names or a nickname.

The next man stepped forward, hat in his hands.

"My name's Cotton, Boss. I take care of the trash for all

the houses and any other little things y'all need. Also do the cleaning, inside and out."

"Do you know anything about rebuilding four-wheeler engines?" Dad asked.

My ears perked up at that.

"No, Boss."

My shoulders slumped. If it was gonna be up to Dad to fix the four-wheeler, I was dead out of luck. But the next man saved my day.

"I know something about engines, Boss."

This man had skin the color of caramel, something I imagined the natives of some faraway tropical island having.

"Have some experience with that?" Dad asked.

"Yes, Boss."

"What's your name?"

"Carlisle, Boss. I'm the gardener. I tend the greenhouse out back."

"A greenhouse. Imagine that," Mom said.

Carlisle nodded respectfully. I noted that he held a different hat than his fellow inmates. While theirs matched their jumpsuits, Carlisle's was white with a yellow bill. He met my eyes, and for a split second, I was sure he looked into my soul. I didn't break eye contact. Dad wouldn't like that; nevertheless, I squirmed inside.

I knew I'd have to avoid this one. I can't explain why. Carlisle wasn't intimidating; it was just . . .

Did you ever get caught doing something you shouldn't be doing? Ever look at their eyes?

"I'd like a walkthrough with each of you in the coming days," Dad said. "We'll figure one another out as we go. As for you two," he was looking at Larry and me, "be respectful, and stay out of the way. You understand?"

I nodded. I knew the rules.

What you have to understand is that there was no chance

anything would or could happen with these inmates because they'd been vetted repeatedly. They were either a lifer or soon getting out. Dad insisted that we were respectful to them at all times like he was. He often told us that they'd done bad things to get in prison, but that they were doing their number, and they were still men, fellow human beings who should be treated like any person out in the world.

"It was very nice to meet you, gentlemen. If there's anything you need, anything that might help this place run a little smoother, you know where to find me."

The staff took this as it was, their dismissal. As the inmates filed out, I breathed easier. I didn't like the way that Carlisle had looked at me. Not at me, *in* me. I shivered and almost startled when Mom touched me on the shoulder.

"Are you okay, James?"

"Yeah, just cold."

She looked at me with that face that told me she knew my mind was elsewhere, however, she didn't pry. That was the good thing about my parents. As long as I painted inside the lines, they pretty much left me to myself. That's exactly why things soon went farther south than Antarctica.

CHAPTER SEVEN

Dinner with the head guards and assistant wardens was more of the same. Dad liked to introduce his family, and no particulars of their jobs were spoken until Larry and I left. That was fine with me, at least until I was out of the room.

Denny Bell had taken the time to remark on how sharp my little brother and I looked.

"You'll be fine young men; you know that."

He didn't tousle our hair or anything like that. He must've known tousling a kid's hair is like serving garlic bread to Dracula. Even then I knew Denny Bell knew a lot more about kids than most adults.

"Come along, boys," Mom said, lifting Larry from his booster seat.

I noted the hush after the polite nods. I hadn't absorbed much of anything during dinner. They'd gone around the table to introduce themselves, but I'd grown weary of introductions. After a while, they all start to blend into one another, and one guy's history belongs to any other guy's past.

The only thing that differs is the name, and that you forget anyway. It was all I could do not to fall asleep in my salad.

I know, of course, hindsight being the nasty little bugger it is, I should've listened. It might have given me the insight that could've prevented what was to come.

"Have a good night, fellas," Denny said. None of the others said a thing.

I dragged my leaden legs to my room, groaning at the thought of having to change into my pajamas.

"Brush your teeth and use the bathroom," Mom said, poking her head in my room.

Like I was going to chew some tobacco and crap the bed. "Okay, Mom."

I don't know how long it took me to get ready, but I'm pretty sure the toothbrush did nothing but make a gentle pass over my teeth. A dentist would be appalled.

"James," I heard Mom say.

"Yeah?"

"Honey, open your eyes."

I did, blinking away the blur.

"I'm ready for bed, Mom."

"Oh?"

There was something in her voice. Amusement?

I blinked through my exhaustion, and that's when I saw it. I was sitting on the toilet, pants down. I'd fallen asleep.

"Get out!" I screamed, scrambling off the pot and re-pantsing myself.

Mom laughed and left me to my embarrassment.

I finished my business, mumbling curses, then washed my hands. It was when I shut off the water that I noticed it. Voices.

Not shouting from the other room. Not whispered like a secret. No, the voices were clear as a bird chirping on the spring wind, and they were coming from the vent next to the bathtub.

I bent down and put my ear to it.

"Jones is a good man. On the other hand, when he's been on a bender, you wanna keep him away from the inmates."

"I'll talk to him." Dad's voice. It sounded like he was taking notes. "Any other delinquents?" I knew what 'delinquents' meant because Dad always said it a certain way, like a magic word that would make terrible monsters appear. It meant nothing good.

"James?" It was Mom calling me from my room.

I knocked my head on the towel rack as I stood.

"Ouch." And muffled, *hell*, *damn*, and a host of other heresies in the crook of my arm.

"Are you okay?"

"I'm okay."

I rubbed my head to ease the pain as I walked into the room. Mom gave me the usual hug and goodnight kiss, waiting for me to get safely under the covers. I had been tired mere minutes before, so much so that I'd made a bed out of the damn commode. But now my mind raced. I had a secret conduit to the dining room that would facilitate the proper execution of one of my favorite pastimes: spying.

CHAPTER EIGHT

The days passed and, pretty much, I was left to myself. I explored as much of the reservation as my legs would allow. It was perfectly safe. At regular intervals, I'd wave to the prison guards rolling by in their battered trucks. The patrols were a mainstay in any prison we lived. It was as natural to me as a passing mailman is to you.

It was one extra hot day that I came across the find of a lifetime. A creek.

To a ten-year-old boy, a creek is Valhalla. It is the alpha and omega of existence. How shall I even begin to explain the wonders of a creek?

And not just any creek. It started ankle deep. Perfect for turning over rocks and finding crawdads. There were places where the water was knee-deep. Not deep enough to swim in, but perfect for sitting down, cooling off, and contemplating life's mysteries.

The water was divinely fresh and cool that day. A fish, the size of my hand, whisked away as I squatted in the deepest place I could find. My head sunk below the creek's bank, invisible to anyone looking from ground level. I turned and crept to the side, grasping the lip as I imagined crawling along by the skirts of the Hudson River as a Revolutionary War sharpshooter, my well-used long rifle in tow.

The prisons where we'd lived employed plenty of military vets. I'd overheard their stories. Some were boastful, like when they talked about going boozing, picking up new friends in what they called a whorehouse. I didn't know what that meant at the time. I assumed it was some kind of community club. I'm glad I wasn't ever asked to join.

Over the preceding years, I'd pieced together the lives of men who'd served in the military, especially the grunts. They had the filthiest mouths and, boy, could they tell a story.

I imagined I was one of them now, creeping along the streambed, slow as summer, keeping my eye out for the top general in the British army. If I could take him out, the war might be over. I'd be a hero.

No general with his entourage appeared though someone else did. It was Harley, our aged groundskeeper. He didn't notice where I was squatting, and that was fine with me. He seemed to be looking for something. His eyes scanned the ground as he moved gingerly through an unruly patch of long grass. Then he bent down and came up again holding something. A huge grin spread over his weathered face. He stuck whatever was in his hand into one of his pockets. Then he moved on, oblivious to my spying eyes.

What had he picked up? A weapon he'd stashed in the grass? Maybe someone on the outside had put it there. Once again, my imagination tore down the path of possibilities. This was my chance to break a case wide open.

I could see the headlines now: "Ten-Year-Old Boy Uncovers Weapon-Smuggling Operation at Federal Prison."

That fertile imagination pushed me to take my first risk in my new home, so I decided to follow Harley. I kept a safe distance, like a smart spy, but a piercing sound dashed my operation. The whistle went off at lunchtime and 5 pm. This shrill sound was the lunch whistle, which meant inmates had to come back to the prison for a headcount. And precisely on cue, Harley turned, ambling his way back to the prison. I noted the bulge in his pocket.

This was it. I'd show my dad that I was worthy of praise. Everyone would talk about the kid who caught a prisoner smuggling a weapon, maybe even a bomb, back into the prison.

"Have a good lunch, Jimmy," Harley said without looking my way.

I popped up, trying to play off my surprise.

I managed to blurt out, "You too, Harley."

I'm not sure, but I think I saw the edges of a smile as he walked away.

Outstanding work, Mr. Bond. Spotted by the weak eyes of a two-hundred-year-old man.

CHAPTER NINE

I didn't let the shame of my uncovering last long. Shaking off the unease that I was spotted so easily, I gave Harley a good cushion of space. There were plenty of trees to hide behind. I kept telling myself that I'd been careless. A simple mistake. He'd probably seen me in the stream long before I'd seen him.

So off I went, tailing the suspect, images in my head of photo-ops with the mayor, maybe even the governor.

"You're a hero, Jimmy," I whispered to myself.

Harley never looked back. He made it all the way to the greenhouse behind our place before he finally did something suspicious. Instead of continuing straight to the prison for lunch headcount, Harley detoured. Then he did something that sealed his fate in my eyes. He looked back once, then again.

"I've got you now, Harley," I said under my breath.

He slipped inside the greenhouse and was back out in no time. It was long enough for him to stash the loot. He moved faster now, on his way back to the stone wall.

I waited for what felt like an eternity. I needed to make

sure Harley was gone. I didn't need two screw-ups in one day. General Washington would never abide such a pitiful spy in his employ.

Patience was not one of my strong suits. Before long, the pull of curiosity and anticipation of heroic accolades got me to the door of the greenhouse. I hadn't been inside—Dad's orders. But Dad was at work, and I was here. Our staff was getting counted with the rest of the inmates. This was my chance. *Do it.*

The greenhouse door creaked like an old lady's hip. My face scrunched in extreme concentration. How did spies deal with squeaky hinges? They probably carried a small can of WD-40 around with them as part of their spy kit. Yeah. I'd have to remember that. I'd have to remind myself to build a spy kit first. Then I would have the WD-40.

I was inside. The humidity of the place was almost too much. Almost. My duty to the prison, no, to my country, pulled me forward. Maybe I'd get a medal. Or my own comic book. A movie. *The Dangerous Adventures of Jimmy Allen.* That sounded good.

The greenhouse seemed larger on the inside. It was roughly the size of our house, with rows and rows of raised garden beds. The only plants I recognized were the tomatoes, the baby fruits plumping up in the regulated heat.

Sweat beaded all over my body. I ignored the discomfort, taking pleasure in the fact that spies of the past had to endure much worse. No water. Little food. Scurvy.

There was a room at the far end of the greenhouse. I snuck that way, glad that the fresh and cool humid earth beneath my feet was soft, and not a sound hit my ears. I made it to the far room and found what looked like a tiny office. There was a cot on one side, a single slab of wood balanced on cinder blocks on the other. Books lay in neat piles on the makeshift desk labeled *Today's Gardening*, *Tomatoes on A Budget*, *Herbs*, and so forth.

This small room had to be Carlisle's domain. He was the greenhouse keeper. What was Harley doing here?

No pictures on the walls. No knickknacks like I'd seen on a rare prison tour. The space was tidy. Too tidy. It was barren of anything personal.

Abandoning all caution, I sat down on the cot, figuring that a good snoop imagined himself in the shoes of a criminal to crack the big case. The bunk was far from comfortable and squeaked under my weight (WD-40 next time!). My feet didn't even touch the ground.

I sat back against the wall, my legs dangling off the edge of the cot, looking all around.

From that angle, I could see things I hadn't at first. Carlisle used the hollow insides of the desk cinder blocks as storage.

Jackpot.

I rose from the cot and closed in on what I knew would be the earth-shattering proof of a prison-wide conspiracy.

The first nook held three empty plastic honey bear bottles. Strange yet not entirely out of place. I've come to know that prisoners hoard all manner of things and are experts in crafting doodads out of scraps. Nothing nefarious in the honey bottles. Just an inmate saving for a rainy day. I moved on.

The next cinder block held a stack of worn paper. I used my shirt to pick up the top bundle. Fingerprints! (I was ignorant of the fact that I'd touched half a zillion things along the way.)

The paper had row upon row of the neatest print I'd ever seen. The handwriting was so immaculate it looked computer-generated. I scoured the notes for escape plans,

guard tower exploitation schemes, or maybe even an assassi-
nation. The list ran like this:

Day 1: melon seeds planted.

Day 4: seedlings sprouted, 2-mm height.

And on and on and on.

So, it was some sort of code.

On second thought, just some boring notes on gardening.

It wasn't until the very last cinder block that I found it,
the proof that would make me a hero in Dad's eyes. First, I
slowly pulled out the wire, careful not to damage or set off
any attachments. This thing had to be dangerous. Why else
would Harley stick it way in the back of the cinder block
hollow?

I tried to steady my breaths, but I'm pretty sure I was
close to hyperventilating.

Then it was out and sitting in my hands: a metal object
the size of a coaster, wires coiled underneath, and a plug on
the backside.

A bomb. I lifted it over my head so I could see underneath.
No C-4 or sticks of dynamite. However, that didn't matter.
This device was a bomb. Had to be.

No sense in tipping my hand now. I was onto Harley *and*
Carlisle.

I had to work this thing carefully. I'd come to Dad with
scant evidence of conspiracies in the past, and he'd been less
than thrilled. There was the garbage caper in Kansas (a
thieving raccoon). The cafeteria theft ring in Wyoming (an
inventory screw-up in the number of fruit cups ordered). But
this . . .

I'd have to build my case. Harley was a mere pawn. A
gofer. A lackey. It was Carlisle; he was the head man. I'd track
his every move. I'd take notes and present them to Dad when
I was ready.

With the nuclear detonator back in its place, I sat back

on the cot and dreamed of glory. I lay back and imagined how Dad would look at me with the same respect he had for his grandfather, my great-grandfather. The legend. He'd served in the First World War, earned all kinds of medals I didn't understand, and then come home to be the first warden in family history. Revered, my great-grandfather, whose name I now wore, went on to do many great things in the federal prison system. He'd broken up riots. He'd saved correctional officers. He'd even met the President.

That's what I wanted. All summed up in one word: GLORY.

I closed my eyes and let the dreams take me. And before long, I was pulled to sleep.

The ace spy at work.

CHAPTER TEN

I've always had vivid dreams. Mom still tells stories about when I was five, and I'd come running at full speed out of my bedroom screaming about dragons or headless knights. Family lore says that the first time I did this, Dad actually pulled a gun thinking a prisoner had somehow snuck into the house. Sorry, Dad, just dragons.

The dream I found myself in now was no different. I could touch every color and savor every taste. This time I was in a green field that stretched as far as the tangerine horizon. I was riding a white stallion, my revolutionary uniform every bit as fit as good old George Washington's. I had a ragged American flag in my left hand. The framed edges snapped in the wind as I rode at full tilt. In my right hand was my ever-present officer's saber, curved like the dragoons of legend. Ah, I was in my element, charging to some as-of-yet unseen foe who likely would be slaughtered with my approach.

A shadow came into view. The silhouette materialized into a man as I got closer. A dark man. He raised his hand like an old friend welcoming me home on a rickety porch. I sensed no danger, and as I approached, I saw no weapons.

The man was familiar; still, I couldn't place him. His face morphed from solid to liquid and then back to solid, and became an amalgamation of faces I'd seen before.

My horse skidded to a stop. Then my imposing steed showed the flare I was famous for on the dream-land battle-field by rearing up on its hind legs with a bellowing neigh. We settled back down to Earth, and the dark man's face had changed again. He was wearing stained overalls, and I could smell the sweat of a long day's work coming off him. I was too polite to wrinkle my nose, so I tipped my hat to him.

"Beautiful horse," the man said. "What's her name?"

"Marauder," I said with authority. "You shouldn't be here." I made my voice blare from deep inside my chest.

The man cocked his head to one side like he was trying to see me better. Then I saw the smile play across his face. "But I live here," he said.

"You live *here?*"

"Of course."

I looked all around the green fields sensing the enemy was coming at any moment. I had to save this delusional man.

"Sir, I'm not sure how you got here, but there are about a billion redcoats headed this way."

All he did was make a chuckle. Then his face solidified for the last time. I knew this man.

"You're . . . I started to say. "

Then some invisible force nudged me backward, nearly toppling me over the back of the horse. I held on strenuously, trying to get an eye on whatever it was that had pushed me.

I tried to speak, but the nudge came again. This one sent me end over end.

I braced for impact, my entire body stiffening, eyes scrunching shut. The hit never came. Nor did I feel the effect of my terrified steed's hooves on my head.

When I opened my eyes, everything was a blur, like I'd

rubbed a greasy hand over a pane of glass. I blinked several times. The blur was darker now, in front of my face. Close.

It was the man looking down at me. But there were no more fields. No more horse. No more sharp uniform.

"You okay?" Carlisle asked, standing with his yellow and white ball cap in his two hands. My mouth moved, yet no words came out like a breached fish dying.

"I think maybe you oughta be getting yourself home," he said.

He didn't have to tell me twice. Dad would kill me if he knew I'd fallen asleep in the greenhouse. In good standing or not, you didn't tread where inmates tread. That's what he liked to say.

I wasn't scared if you can believe that. I'd never been scared of the inmates. At least not the ones that were working at our home. But the heat, the dream, the new place, all of it thrown together put me in the middle of some mushy stew of fear and distrust.

I whipped up onto my feet, ready to run from the greenhouse. My head reeled.

"Hey, you okay?"

I'd heard that question before, hadn't I?

I put out a hand to show Carlisle. "I'm . . ."

That's when my world tilted again, and all I remember was Carlisle's face hovering before mine. Things went dark and quiet after that.

CHAPTER ELEVEN

I finally woke, screaming; I had no idea where I was. I'm not proud of it. I cried like I was five. It was dark, and the smells were new. Was I in a dungeon? Had I been captured on the battlefield?

A light flashed on overhead, and I had to shield my eyes from the blinding glare.

"James."

"Mom?"

"Honey, are you okay?"

Big question. I wasn't okay. My head felt like my imaginary stallion had kicked it.

"What happened?"

"You passed out. Carlisle brought you home."

"Carlisle," I said in wonder.

"How many times have I told you to make sure you drink enough water? You were dehydrated, silly. It was lucky for you that Carlisle found you."

Dehydrated? That would explain some things. I'd been on the edge of dehydration before. Once at the age of seven, I went exploring the new reservation. I'd chased a rabbit. It had to have been a half a mile. I remembered panting in the hot sun, the searing thirst, and the realization that I hadn't had any water the whole morning.

I didn't feel thirsty now, just worn down. Like I'd run a marathon, barefooted, with a hundred-pound pack on and a vice clamp on each knee.

"We had to call the doctor. He put some fluids in." Her hand brushed over my forearm and stopped on something—a bandage.

"They put a needle in me?"

Mom nodded. "You didn't squirm at all. Nevertheless, it took a couple of sticks."

I was brave about a lot of things. Needles were not one of them. There'd been more than one occasion when I'd bolted from a doctor's office only to be found an hour later in some janitor's closet. I remember sitting in there vowing to belt the next doc in the nose who tried to stab me with one of those evil things.

"Am I gonna be okay?"

"Of course, honey. You need to take better care of yourself on these hot days."

WD-40 and a canteen. Duly noted.

Mom stroked my forehead. Her hand was perfectly cool and soothing, a tonic I'd remember in later years.

"When can I go play?"

Mom laughed. "It's nighttime, James."

"What?"

How long had I been out?

"Why don't you rest, honey? I'll bring you some dinner if you're hungry."

At the mention of food, my stomach grumbled loud enough for Mom to hear.

"I'll take that as a yes," she said. "A grilled cheese, okay?"

Grilled cheese, okay? Does the Pope sprinkle holy water on his Cheerios?

"Yes, please," I said, trying to still the tsunami of saliva in my mouth.

Mom passed her thumb over my cheek.

"Okay. You relax. Dinner in ten minutes."

After she left the room, it wasn't long before I was only half-thinking about grilled cheese. The other half of me was thinking about my dream and why Carlisle had been in it. That never had and would never happen again. You wake up from a dream, and there's the person you were talking to on the other side.

The other side, I thought to myself.

I'd need to think about what it all meant.

CHAPTER TWELVE

I couldn't gather the nerve to approach the greenhouse for another three days. I saw Carlisle but avoided his gaze awkwardly, like a guy who'd been caught doing something unbiblical in a girls' locker room. I'm glad he didn't say anything to me. I'm not sure what I would've said back.

That didn't mean I didn't watch him. Like the spy I wanted to be, I hid behind trees, in gullies and along creek beds, always watching. I noticed things I hadn't before. The rotation of the guards. The coming and going of the inmates who worked in staff housing. The same flocks of birds that seemed to show up at the same time every day to snack on worms, bugs, or the bits of bread I'd bring from home.

Dad never said anything about my fainting. Health concerns were Mom's domain. It was apparent that I was not in any trouble. I wondered if Dad even knew I'd fallen asleep in the greenhouse, oblivious to the world. Afterward, when I was feeling better, I didn't get a whooping.

It didn't make any sense. Time to figure out the mystery.

So, one day at lunch, I chattered away as Mom only half listened. I was doing my best to recite what I'd read the night before in my latest Captain America comic. The old lady was hooked. That's when I sprung the question.

"Hey, Mom? Where did Carlisle find me when I passed out?"

Boom. From Cap to Carlisle in twelve seconds flat.

"Ooooh," Larry said.

I threw him a dirty look.

"I told you," Mom answered, not looking up from the magazine she was reading.

"No, you didn't."

"I didn't?"

"Mom . . ." I waited for her to look up.

"What is it, honey?"

I had a plan. All great spies have plans.

"I think I dropped one of my G.I. Joes. I can't find it. I thought it might be where Carlisle found me."

Total lie, yet Mom bought it whole hog.

"I'm pretty sure he said it was in the fields. I'm not sure where. Maybe you should ask him."

That was my cue. Lunch was forgotten, and I sped out of the room. Mom had given me permission to interrogate.

Carlisle, the bell tolls for thee.

CHAPTER THIRTEEN

I found him in the greenhouse. It wasn't precisely a recon mission. Other than the odd helping hand he lent to other inmates; his life *was* that greenhouse. Everything was neat and in its place.

He was wearing his hat when I found him. It was the first time I noticed that it was spotless. Not a speck of dirt. Not a ring of old sweat. In a place where earth and sweat were as common as the flowers they produced, I found that odd.

It was also the first time I noticed faded letters on the front of the ball cap: S.D. Another mystery.

He was in the middle of shoveling dirt from an old wheelbarrow into a bucket when I made my appearance. I'd been watching him for a good ten minutes.

"Whatcha doing?" I asked as casually as could be.

Carlisle looked up from another shovel full, squinting in the sun.

"Just bringing in some good dirt."

"Good dirt?"

He nodded. "Yep. There's good dirt, and there's bad dirt. Found a good patch down that way." He motioned with his index finger to the fields that were my playground. "Right mix for the plants to grow. I think it used to be a cow pasture."

He patted down the bucket of dirt then stretched up to his full height. Carlisle wasn't a tall man, not like some of the guards I'd met, but the way he stretched made me think that he could touch heaven if he wanted to.

"So, is it cow poop?" I asked, immediately chiding myself for sounding so juvenile. I knew it was called manure.

He chuckled. "I'm no expert. Just know what makes the plants grow."

We stood there for what seemed like an hour. It was probably thirty seconds. I started to sweat through my shirt; however, Carlisle didn't look the least bit uncomfortable.

Finally, I mustered up the nerve. "Can I see the plants?"

He shook his head slowly. "Don't know if that's a good idea."

"It's okay. My mom knows I'm talking to you."

Now he looked at me. Like, *really* looked at me.

"Did you need to talk to me about something?"

Here it was. Tell the truth or lie? I was better at the latter when under interrogation.

But this was *my* interrogation, dammit. I needed answers.

"Why did you tell my parents you found me in the fields?"

I'd attempted to dart him with a verbal dagger; instead, it'd sounded like a slurpy noodle coming out. Didn't matter. It was out in the open, and I was happy to see his face scrunched in thought.

"Well, I guess I thought you might get in trouble."

"In trouble?"

"Sure. For falling asleep in the greenhouse."

Maybe so, Carlisle. Or perhaps you didn't want my dad to inspect the greenhouse. Could be I'd been on the right trail after all. Come clean, Carlisle. You're hiding something, aren't you? What is it? A knife? A gun? A bomb? I got you dead to rights, Carlisle. You're sunk.

That's something a better interrogator, one who didn't have a mouth full of marbles and a brain-full of Sugar Pops, would say.

Instead, I said, "You were afraid of getting in trouble."

Okay, not the pithiest of phrases, but it came out the way I wanted, like an accusation.

He did his grave nod again. I had him now.

"I can see how you might think that; still, this is my greenhouse. I'm allowed to be in there. You're not."

Shoot. Carlisle was three steps ahead. I felt my hold on the subject slipping.

"But I'm a kid," I countered. "You could've gotten in trouble for having a kid in the greenhouse."

I'd heard the nasty things mean inmates did to kids, like touching them in places and stuff like that. I'd seen their eyes, the bad ones. They weren't the same as Carlisle's.

Again, the nod. Slow. Thoughtful. "I can see how that might happen. Is that really what's bothering you? That I could've gotten in trouble?"

Dammit. Carlisle was twisting my words again, using them against me. Buckle down, Jimmy. What would General Washington do against a wily double agent?

"Why did you help me?" I said, sounding like the ten-year-old I was.

Nod. Smile.

"You're a good kid, Jimmy. But you're adventurous. I mean, what kid your age isn't? All the same, there ain't no use getting in trouble the first week you're here, right?"

He smiled as if he'd been in my shoes.

I nodded without thinking, without realizing I was mimicking the gravity of the act.

"Besides," he said, "I think God's got a plan for you, Jimmy."

That struck me like a barn door in the face. "What's God got to do with it?"

The Allen family could in no way be called devout; anyhow, I knew enough not to bring up God in idle conversation, or, God forbid, use his name in vain. Dad never went to church with us, but he drew the line at cursing God. That was enough to get your mouth washed out with soap, or worse, whooped good.

Again, that languid smile, like he'd seen every inch of the world and knew all the wrinkles he could balance on.

"God's got *everything* to do with it." He looked from the ground to the sky like that was enough explanation.

"*James!*"

I ignored Mom's call. Stared down Carlisle instead, waiting for further explanation. But he was still looking up at the sky.

"*James! Time to go!*"

I rolled my eyes. "Coming, Mom!" Then to Carlisle. "Thanks."

"Thanks? For what?"

"For helping me."

He looked straight into me. It didn't feel so foreign this time.

"My pleasure, Jimmy. Come around any time, as long as it's okay with your parents."

I nodded, humbled by his invitation.

As I walked away, I felt as discombobulated as I had after a spin on the Whirling Dervish at the old county fair in New York.

CHAPTER FOURTEEN

"Rockstar" might not be the technical term for what Dad was, nevertheless that's what he was. We knew so because of the praises we'd heard about him. If they'd never reached our ears, we might have thought Dad some schlub lost in bureaucratic shuffling of personnel throughout the country. He never spoke of why they wanted him in so many places. It wasn't because he was the youngest federal prison warden in the U.S., although he was that too. No, they wanted him because Dad was what you might call a "fixer." That's not a technical term either.

Say a prison has a problem, anything from gangs, a booming drug trade, to incompetence—they send in Dad. He breaks up the gangs, sending members to opposite sides of the country. He crushes drug running by setting up new systems, changing up the schedule, anything to keep offending inmates on their toes. A bored inmate is a liability, he says, and so he keeps them busy. And like a shark always in motion to stay alive, Dad charges ahead, fixing and moving, his wake a swirling tendril of order.

We couldn't have been in Virginia more than a couple of

weeks when the first changes rolled in. First, I noticed one guard, then another, take their final walk out of prison. Then the prison buses started rolling in and carting off select prisoners by the half-dozen.

New faces appeared. New guards. New prisoners. Soon another dinner where I'd man my perch in the bathroom and listen in for information.

Back then, when my imagination revved on the tiniest stimulant, I thought there was always the chance I might overhear some lurid detail about some inmate's behavior, perhaps some gratuitous gore, or better yet, a blow-by-blow account of a riot or jailbreak.

The dinner came. I remember it in perfect detail.

Three guards showed up in suits. Wearing a suit and tie was expected at a dinner with the warden. This was official. I'll bet some of them never wore those suits again until they buried a friend or got buried themselves. I remember seeing one guard with a sales tag sticking out of his pants leg.

They showed up five minutes early. They'd gotten the memo. The first two guards were as vanilla as guards went. They were young and eager and too new to know the difference.

The third . . . how can I put this? He was a muscle covered in freckles, all topped off with a mound of curly red hair—Alfred E. Neuman on steroids.

After shaking Dad's hand, he reached a hand down to me.

"Evening, little buddy," he sang. His voice was slick and phony.

"James, this is Brady Bruce."

Even his name sounded fake, like a superhero alias.

"It's a pleasure to meet you, Mr. Bruce," I said just like I'd been taught. Firm handshake. Look a man in the eye. Dad's training had become part of my musculature.

"Firm handshake you got there, little buddy."

The first iteration of 'little buddy' was annoying. Now it was like a dull razor blade scraping down my arm. I tried to let go of his hand. He wouldn't let it go.

"It sure is nice of your parents to have us to dinner."

I tried to pull away. Dad didn't notice because he was talking to the other guards. My body was threatening to go into panic mode, and my brain scrambled for something to do. Be strong like Dad. This man with his fake, oiled voice wasn't going to mess with me.

"Can I get you a beer, Mr. Bruce?"

At that, he brightened, spell broken.

"Don't mind if you do." He pointed at me and winked. I choked back vomit.

I could tell by his brief scowl that Dad had heard that one. Mom reserved the beer for guests we knew.

"I'll be right back, Mr. Bruce," I said, Johnny-on-the-spot.

I skittered into the kitchen, quick to wash my hands, twice. It felt like it wasn't enough. There was something about Brady Bruce that I didn't like.

Did you ever touch a cockroach? For a long time after, you can't shake the feeling that you shouldn't have.

CHAPTER FIFTEEN

Dinner was a bust. I sat in the bathroom the entire time, head next to my listening vent.

Dad talked about his expectations and where he saw the prison going in the coming months. He didn't blather. Straight to the point. He never discussed details that weren't needed.

There were one or two times when Brady Bruce chimed in. I stiffened at the sound of his voice, hoping I'd hear Dad jump up from the table and fire him on the spot.

But that didn't happen. Instead, Bruce droned on for minutes about his old prisons. There was a lot of kissing up in his storytelling, and that made me dislike him even more.

"You would've liked Pennsylvania, Warden," he said. "Best darned peach cobbler in the system. No offense to Mrs. Allen." I could hear the wink.

And that's how it went. No secrets. No orders. Just business.

By the time they finished dinner and said their goodbyes, I was on my way to bed, yawning the whole way.

I was midway through another yawn, eyes closed, when I ran into someone.

My eyes snapped open, fully awake now.

"Hey there, little buddy!"

He reached down and did the dreaded tousle of hair. I was too tired to punch him in the nuts.

"Headed to bed?" he asked when he finished the tousling.

No genius, I'm going to meet the President.

I nodded like a deaf-mute. Bruce looked around appreciatively. "Nice place you guys got here." Then, for the first time, I heard the bite in his voice. That bitter tinge that I'd come to identify as his calling card. "Sure would be nice if I could have a place like this."

His eyes flashed with enough animosity to make me take a step back. And just like that, it was gone. Back to syrupy niceness.

"Hey, I'm sorry, little buddy." Like he realized he'd let the mask slip. "I was looking for the bathroom."

"Back there," I said.

"Thanks. Hey, you didn't stink up the place, did you?" The point and the wink again.

He chuckled and loped off. I stood at the spot in concrete shoes. In the briefest encounter, Brady Bruce had somehow defiled our home. I tried to shake it off as I got changed for bed and tried to push away the dread as I clicked off the light. I didn't wish to slip into those dreams.

But when I finally got to the core of my "imaginative state," Brady Bruce was there waiting, smiling, beckoning. The wink. The tousle of hair. The mask of niceness. The goop in the voice. This night would belong to Brady Bruce.

CHAPTER SIXTEEN

The next morning, I was dragging like an old hound dog. I should've stayed in bed. It was summer, and Mom wouldn't have cared. But that would've given the win to the baby-faced guard of my latest nightmare. Brady Bruce's *look* had unnerved me. Even when I first met him, his face looked like an oversized baby. I get it. Babies are cute. On the other hand, take that kind of face and blow it up to the size of an adult, and you have yourself something quite hideous to behold. All bulging muscle under his suit and baby face up top.

I shuffled my way to the kitchen, barely acknowledging Mom. Then I plopped into my customary seat at the table and began shoveling cereal into my mouth like I was clearing rubble.

As I was going in for my last bite, Mom finally chimed in. "How did you sleep, honey?"

"Okay."

She didn't look up from her book, or she'd have seen my frown.

"Big plans for today?"

"Just going outside."

She lowered the book. "I have to go to the store, say in an hour. Do you want to come?"

My ears perked up at the question. Body juices flowing to my brain. "Can we go to the toy store?"

I'd been planning the run. There was a list of things I needed.

"Only the grocery store, this time."

I slumped back into my chair. "Nah, I'll stay here."

"You sure? We could get ice cream?"

Not even ice cream, that Prozac of the spirit, could lift me out of my funk that day.

"No thanks," I said, and rose from the table to take my cereal bowl to the sink.

"Okay," Mom said. "But if you're staying home, I need you to keep Larry."

Not even ice cream . . .

"Come on, Mom," I whined.

"You'll be fine, James. Let him tag along."

I couldn't understand why Larry needed a chaperone, what with roving patrols going by every ten minutes, neighbors within earshot, and staff inmates outside.

"Mom," I said, intonation like I was casting a spell.

"Now, James. I haven't asked you since we moved in. Besides, it'd be good to spend time with your brother. He wants to be like you, you know."

Of course, I knew that. It's one of the things I hated about my little brother.

"Fine," I said.

"Good. I'll leave lunch just in case I'm gone longer."

Just like that, my planned day of finding a sweet shady spot outside in which I'd fall asleep to the sounds of nature was dashed. Babysitting. I was no babysitter. I wasn't even going to get paid for it!

Mom checked in before she left, Larry on her heels.

"You two be nice to each other, okay?"

Larry rushed into my room. He picked up two G.I. Joes that were locked in a death match wrestle move.

"Hey, don't touch!" I yelled.

"You boys have fun," Mom said, already on her way to the front door.

I watched Larry for a while, too tired to make him stop defiling my possessions with his snotty fingers and polluting my room with his presence. I should've gotten back into bed and closed my eyes. That would have been the "smart" thing to do. So would faking a coma. But after all, I didn't always pick the smart thing to do.

"Jimmmmmy?"

The whine made me itch all over.

"What is it, brat?"

"Want to go outside?"

To give him credit, Larry had put the G.I. Joes back in their previous death-match positions. Now he stood there, dancing in place like I was holding him up.

"Fine. Let me get changed."

Larry didn't leave.

"You gonna watch me, pervert?"

"What's a 'pervert'?"

"It's a boy who likes to wear dresses and eat slugs."

Larry rushed from the room and closed the door dutifully.

"Well, what now?" I asked to the air as I slipped out of my pajamas and into my play clothes.

That's when the idea came. In hindsight, the plan was ill-timed and wasn't thought-out.

"Hey, Larry!"

"Yeeaahhhh?"

"Wanna play in the fort?"

"Yeah!"

Little did I know that his exuberance to tag along would be my first real mistake in Virginia. A real doozy.

CHAPTER SEVENTEEN

When we stepped outside, the muggy summer day was in a high hitch. It swooped down on us like a dousing of warm water.

Larry ran out the door, seemingly oblivious to the heat. He had a bucket of army men in his hand.

"Come on, Jimmy!"

"Yeah, yeah. Keep your diaper on."

It was cooler in the cabin fort, but not by much. My head was already itching with prickling sweat when I stepped inside.

By the time our first round of playing hide and seek was done, my back was soaked. My idea was also seeping away. Maybe a day inside with air conditioning would be better.

"I'm the good guy. You're the bad guy," Larry said, tagging me and running into the next room of the fort.

An exaggerated sigh left my lips. Then I perked up at the thought of soaking my feet in the refreshing stream.

"Alright," I said, "you go hide, and I'll find you. Don't come out until I find you, okay?"

"Okay!" came Larry's muffled voice from around the corner.

I counted to twenty out loud. And then, "Ready or not, here I come!"

I made a real production of stomping around. I knew where Larry had gone.

"Man, where is he?" I asked aloud, stomping around some more, huffing and puffing like a method actor. That went on for another couple of minutes. Then I put the crux of my plan in place, padding to the front door as quietly as I could.

I gave an Oscar-worthy, "Man, Larry sure is good playing hide-and-seek," and then I was outside.

Figuring it was best to make sure he didn't go anywhere; I locked the latch. Larry would be safe for the few minutes I was away getting some peace and quiet.

My first stop was the creek, and oh, was the water gloriously cold. I don't know how long I sat there savoring the feel up to my knees. But the sun had moved, and an annoying ray was hitting me square in the back. That wouldn't do. So, I slipped under a tree that looked like it'd been tailor-made to my size. I mean, it had one of those curved nooks and everything. I slid into it like it was a La-Z-Boy, savoring every inch of the shade. Ah, this was the good life. Free of annoyance. Free of responsibility. Free.

I figured I'd close my eyes for a few and then go back to fetch Larry. A neon sign in my head had buzzed to life and was blaring brightly. It said: LUNCH.

When my eyes shut, I went straight to my dreams. Pleasant dreams this time, thankfully. No Brady Bruce and his bobblehead terror.

I was returning from the second Battle at Saratoga, having forced Burgoyne's men to retreat and Burgoyne to surrender. When asked why he did so, he said, "It was that Allen kid. He wouldn't let up."

As I marched back to town, I heard the people cheering. The celebration for the return of their war hero was beginning.

That was off in the distance. Here, it was only me and my two friends, Peace and Quiet.

———

THE SCREAM RIPPED me from my serenity.

"Help!"

I was still coming out of my trance, however awake enough to be cognizant of the fact that the sun had moved even more.

"Help me! Oh, my baby!"

That was Mom.

I bolted from the tree, leaving my shoes behind. Thoughts of evil inmates ripping my mom to shreds flashed through me. I had no idea what I would do, but when you hear that sound, that utter terror from someone you know to be steadfast and not prone to exaggeration, it sends a shiver of cold through you so thoroughly that you either run away or run towards it.

I made it to the greenhouse just as Carlisle was emerging. He matched my pace immediately.

"You know what's going on?" he asked as we ran.

"Mom," was all I said. The heat was pressing, and my adrenaline was starting to wane. I could feel that familiar lightheadedness driving in.

That's when it hit me.

Larry.

Of all the stupid things I could've done.

We found Mom at the door of the fort. She was sitting in the grass, her back to us.

"Mrs. Allen?" Carlisle asked, panting.

Mom's head whipped around, and that's when I saw him. He was limp in her arms, face pale and slack.

I skidded to a stop with a thousand and one excuses coming to mind.

"James, what—"

"Mrs. Allen, is it okay if I take a look at him?" Carlisle asked, going down to one knee, still careful to leave some distance between them.

Her eyes, rimmed with red and soaked with terrified tears, went from me to Carlisle.

"Please help him," she pleaded.

Carlisle bent closer. I couldn't see what he did, and it was only a few seconds before he said, "We should take him to the dispensary."

"In the prison?"

"Yes, ma'am. Here, why don't you give your son to me?"

With only a bit of reluctance, Mom handed Larry over.

He was dead. He had to be dead. At that moment, I prayed to God as I'd never prayed to him before.

God, please help my brother. God, please help my brother.

Carlisle didn't waste any time. He was up and running, and it was all I could do to keep up. Mom fell behind and was out of sight by the time we got to the gate.

"What the hell is this?" the guard asked, wiping sweat from his brow with a handkerchief.

"It's the Allen boy, Boss. We need to take him to the infirmary."

"Hold it, not on my—"

"Look, Boss, you don't want it on your head if something happens to the warden's boy." Then, in a calm voice that was heavy with authority, he said, "I'm taking this boy inside. Now you want to call someone to escort us, or should I do it myself?"

I could see the wheels spinning in the guard's head. That's when my mother appeared.

"Let us in," she said, her voice wracked.

That was all it took. The guard nodded, and Carlisle was off again.

What came next is sort of a blur. I remember getting to the small clinic. The stares. The curiosity.

Then the doctor showed up. He was young. Even I knew that at the time. But he had kind eyes, and he told Carlisle where to put Larry. Then the doctor noticed me.

"I think you should take the boy out," he said, not unkindly.

I didn't want to go, but Carlisle said I should.

"Don't worry. We'll stay with your brother."

The full weight of what I'd done had finally sunk in. I had killed my own brother. Me and my two friends: Peace and Quiet. I felt like crap. Low down dirty devil cursed crap.

I looked up at Carlisle, my eyes brimming with tears. "How do you know he'll be okay?"

"I know. Now you go. I'll come and find you when it's okay."

There wasn't anything else to do. An orderly escorted me out of the examination area and scrounged up a chair for me to sit in. I think he asked me some questions. All I remember is shaking my head, over and over again. Anyhow, it wasn't in response to the orderly. I was lashing myself every which way I could. And through it, one word clanged like an iron bell in my mind: *murderer*.

CHAPTER EIGHTEEN

Dad marched in at some point trailed by Denny Bell. Dad didn't even glance at me. Denny threw me a look like what I imagined a condemned man might get from a sympathetic executioner.

I went deep with my depression. I'd never experienced loss before, not a real loss. Unless you count the dog that we found when I was five, the one that got into a box of rat poison three weeks later.

I found myself wishing for Larry's little foibles. Like the way he always wanted to play with me; he'd find a pretty flower and bring it to me. The first few times, I pretended to be appreciative. After a while I began tossing them in the can, telling Larry you're only supposed to bring flowers to girls.

I wanted to take it all back. Every jab. Every taunt. Every mean word.

It was Carlisle who came to fetch me. Not Mom. Not Dad. Carlisle.

"They say you can come," he said, looking down at me.

"Carlisle, I thought . . . I didn't . . .

"Shhh. It's okay."

How could it be okay? I'd killed my brother. How would that be okay?

I got up from the plastic chair and skulked in behind Carlisle. My feet were as heavy as my heart. *I'm sorry, Larry.*

"Jimmy," I heard someone croak.

I peeked around the curtain and saw him. Not slack with death. Pale, sure, but very much alive and looking for me.

Pushing past the doctor, I ran to him.

Tubes were running into his arm, and I avoided them to give him an awkward hug.

"I'm sorry, Larry." I held on to him so hard. *So hard.*

"Ow," he said. "Stop. You're only supposed to hug girls!"

I guess I taught him a little too well. I didn't care, though I eased up.

"I'm sorry," I said again. Then the realization of the adults watching the "Jimmy Show" sunk in. I slunk back from the bed.

"What happened?" Larry asked me. Of course, he asked me. He always asked me his questions first.

I fumbled for an answer.

"We'll talk about it later," Dad said.

Larry was alive. I was dead meat.

CHAPTER NINETEEN

No one said a word to me when we walked home. No one told me to go to my room, but I went like a guilty man. No dinner was offered. No orders came to put on my pajamas. No goodnight kisses. Ten years old and put in solitary confinement.

I heard them put Larry to bed and heard Mom tell Larry how much she loved him. I also heard Dad make a rare appearance telling Larry how brave he'd been.

Then they both went to the kitchen. So, I slipped to the bathroom to my listening vent. If I was going to get a whooping, I wanted to know when it was coming.

"How could this happen?" Dad said. "Weren't you watching them?"

If Dad thought Mom was going to lie down and take it, he was wrong.

"I went to the store. I've gone to the store before. James was in charge. He made a mistake."

"A mistake?"

"Yes, a mistake. Humans make them."

"And I assume you expect me to look the other way."

"I didn't say that."

"But it's what you want, isn't it?"

"Dean, why don't you take off your warden's cap for a night. He is your son."

There was a pause. "What the hell is that supposed to mean?" There was a scary softness in Dad's anger now.

"It means that you treat the boys, especially James, the way you treat the guards. I can't remember the last time you hugged him. If *I* can't remember it . . ."

Dad's voice was low now. I had to strain to hear it.

"You think I should hug him? For what? Leaving his brother to die of a heat stroke?"

"He didn't die, Dean. Did you ever think about how James might be feeling? What—do you think he's happy about this? You have two sons. It would be good if you remembered that."

"I didn't get where I am by having my father coddle me."

"Oh," Mom exclaimed in exaggeration. "God forbid a man should show some affection to a child!"

"Don't start with me, Esther."

Another pause. The sound of dishes clinking in the sink.

"A child, Dean—a *boy*—needs love from his father."

"He knows that I love him."

I figured Mom had magic powers to make Dad say that.

The sound of a lighter flicking and the ensuing pause, then the exhale.

"What do you want from me, Esther?"

"I want you to be a father."

Dad's voice slipped into the barest modicum of resignation. "Esther."

"Dean, you discipline James the way you think is best. I won't get in your way." My throat constricted. "But for heaven's sake, be fair. Be a *father*."

"When am I ever mean, even with the inmates?"

Mom sighed. "Your son is not an inmate."

There was a pause, and Dad said, "No, and he won't be."

And then a long pause. The conversation was over. I slipped from the bathroom, into my room, and under the covers. It didn't take long, though it felt like a millennium. My door creaked open, and Dad stepped inside. The light in the hallway silhouetted his form.

"Get up, son."

I did as I was told, quick to get on my feet. I'd been through this before. Dad would order me to bend over the bed or reach down and grab my ankles. No wooden spoon in his hand, so it was going to be *old school*: his calloused mitt.

"I'm sorry, Dad."

He didn't say a thing for a long time. I couldn't see his face in the dark.

"Come on," he said, then turned and headed the opposite way.

I followed him, past the kitchen where Mom was still washing the dishes from a dinner I hadn't eaten. Out the front door. Past the now-infamous fort and around the back of the house.

Dad opened the greenhouse door and flicked on a light. Why were we going to the greenhouse? Maybe it was only going to be a talk. Hope fluttered somewhere between my belly button and my heart.

I stepped in as he moved deeper inside, towards Carlisle's little office.

"Close the door, James."

I closed the door. I took a breath. I kept walking.

I felt the dirt under my bare feet, wishing I could sink down into it.

Yes. A talk. That had to be it. A whooping happened at home. Courage bubbled up inside of me, and my steps became more confident.

Yes. Like a truce in the middle of a battlefield with two generals meeting to discuss a mutually beneficial way forward.

"Hurry up, James."

Dad's voice had that mellow tone I'd heard before. The one reserved for awkward conversations. Like the time he'd invited me out to throw the football, only to use it as a segue to tell me about sex. How he'd made the topic leap from forward passes to intercourse was positively artistic.

He usually lit up a cigarette during these manly heart-to-hearts. Why wasn't he pulling out his Lucky Strikes?

We were in Carlisle's office now. Nowhere to go. Something came out of Dad's pocket. I recognized it as one of the hundred white handkerchiefs he had in his collection. He carried one or two every day, especially in the summer.

He did something with it I'd never seen him do. He stretched it out lengthwise, corner to corner, then he spun it around itself in a twisted spool, like you do when you're about to smack someone with a towel. Then he folded it over on itself.

"Open your mouth," he said, turning to me, the handkerchief held out.

"Sir?"

I reserved my most respectful retorts for when I was in really deep doo. This felt like one of those times. I felt like I was going to throw up.

"Open your mouth and bite down on this, James."

The handkerchief came closer. I could smell Mom's laundry detergent.

"But, Dad . . ."

His eyes went hard. I knew that look. No words needed.

I opened my mouth, and he stuck in the handkerchief like a horse's bit.

"Bite down."

I bit down, still not understanding.

Dad unbuckled his belt.

My knees rattled. Bile crept up my throat; I was going to choke. I let a small whine escape from my throat.

The belt came off, and Dad pointed to the cinder block desk.

"Grab hold." And then, as if he was somehow helping me, he said, "It's okay if you scream. The handkerchief will muffle the sound."

I threw Dad one last pleading look. I was too shocked to cry even though I desperately wanted to. Maybe tears would veer him from this path.

"Put your hands on the edge of the desk."

I complied. No complaining now. No sense running either. Both would only make things worse. I'm not sure how they could've gotten worse, but Dad would figure it out if it were possible.

I was bent at the waist.

No warning.

The first belt whip shocked me to silence. The pain wasn't immediate, and I thought that maybe I was too tough to feel it.

Negative. The pain came. Burning. Stinging. Toe-tingling pain.

The second slap brought the tears. I watched as they dropped down onto the desk, soaking a corner of one of Carlisle's note sheets.

The third whip made me scream. I don't know where it came from, my inner being probably. Dad was right; the handkerchief muffled the sound. I felt my spit soaking it.

The hits to my rear came harder now, faster.

And through it all, I screamed.

I screamed, and I cried, and I lost myself to the pain.

CHAPTER TWENTY

I didn't get out of bed the next morning. Mom had seen me drag myself in behind Dad the night before. It was long after Dad left for work that Mom came in with a tray of breakfast, the one reserved for sick days.

"I made chocolate chip pancakes," she said. "And bacon. I can make more if you want it."

Chocolate chip pancakes were my favorite, and she knew it.

"I'm not hungry."

I kept staring at the ceiling, just like I had been for the entire night. I'd contemplated every conceivable option available to a ten-year-old. From sneaking into Dad's room and whooping him with my own belt to running away. In the end, I opted to stay in bed, staring at blotches on the ceiling, twisting them into Rorschach shapes. I was humbled, a bold lion showed that there was something much stronger than itself.

"I'll leave it here," Mom said, placing the tray on my nightstand.

I ignored her, and I kept ignoring her the entire day. She'd left her cub to a rabid wolf. I knew she saw that. On the other hand, what could she do?

Nothing.

And I did nothing. Nothing except stare up at the ceiling and wait for the pain in my backside to subside.

CHAPTER TWENTY-ONE

I don't remember how many days it took me to crawl from my cave. It was inevitable that I'd get hungry at some point. Mom wouldn't let me lie in my body stink for too long. To me, it seemed like a month. It was probably a day and a half, maybe two.

When I emerged from my self-imposed cell, I felt like a changed man. Yes, a man. I know it sounds ridiculous. Maybe it was. But that's what happens when you catch a glimpse of the shadow side of people you trust.

I'd never been on the butt-end of that level of execution-style punishment, and something in me had broken. The warden was my father, the man who'd given me part of my life, who provided a roof over my head. Now he was little more than some sadistic landlord.

The second was Mom. What happens to a boy when his life-giver gives the okay to have his flesh flayed off?

Last, there was me. The pain and the ensuing self-analysis skinned the childhood from my being.

The only positive thing I had was aimed toward Larry. Never would I hurt him again.

The less visible part of me took a more twisted turn. I'd had my nerve endings burned with hellfire, and now they were numb. They'd callous over soon. The near-death of Larry, the argument between my parents, and the subsequent thrashing in the greenhouse had worked in awful confluence to reform me.

Of course, time would heal a portion of those thoughts and ease them into some long-forgotten memory. Although not all of it.

IT WAS on the day of my willing release that I left the house with Larry. He would be my constant companion going forward. We spent time splashing around the creek, climbing the lowest tree limbs that could hold our combined weight. I boosted him up, and he grunted like he was climbing Mount Kilimanjaro.

I have to give Larry credit here. Whether he didn't remember or was too young to be bitter, he never once mentioned the fort incident. He seemed to latch onto my changed attitude. It was like we'd grown up together. He listened to my directions and rarely ever acted like an annoying five-year-old in my presence again. The perfect little gentlemen companion. The Billy Lee to my General Washington.

The whistle for midday headcount blew, and we watched as the trustees left what I called "the free zone."

Harley chatted along with Cotton while Carlisle brought up the rear. He was reading a book as he walked.

"Carlisle's nice," Larry said, flicking an ant off his leg.

"Mmm," I said.

These were the long days of summer in my childhood when small philosophies stretched like our shadows.

THAT NIGHT, Dad wasn't home for dinner. Mom looked anxious. She even spilled Larry's milk when she reached across the table to put another roll on his plate.

"I'm sorry, Larry," she murmured.

Larry didn't care that she'd spilled the glass right onto his lap. He laughed like he'd been down a water ride at Kings Dominion.

I helped Mom clean up the mess and then took the soaking napkins to the laundry room. When I passed the window, I stopped and stared out.

Strange.

It looked like every prison light was on: one big beacon of dazzling brightness. That was new. So much brilliance at once.

That's when it hit me. We hadn't heard the second whistle for evening headcount. Carlisle and the others hadn't come back to work. Larry and I had gone on playing without noticing a thing.

I chucked the soiled napkins in the washing machine and marched back into the kitchen.

"Something's happening at the prison," I said.

Larry perked up. "What is it? A riot?" He'd learned the word. He had no idea what it meant.

Mom threw me a look. "It's fine. Just emergency drills." She picked up her still-full plate and scraped its contents into the trash with a knife. "James, would you please help me with the dishes?"

"But, Mom . . ."

"James?" She held out the plate.

When I was standing next to her, she whispered so only I could hear. "Your father said we should stay in the house."

"Why?"

She looked over at Larry, who was busy making a rocket ship out of his fork and whispered,

"A prisoner is missing."

"Really?" I wasn't scared in the least. Dad had always told us that when a prisoner disappears, he usually wants to get as far away from the prison as quickly as he can. This was more like an adventure than something to worry over.

She put a finger to her lips.

A knock at the front door made us both jump up.

"Mrs. Allen?" came a voice.

"Denny!" Larry said and hopped up from the table. I wasn't the only fan of the assistant warden with the movie star looks.

Mom opened the door, and Denny Bell stood there with a walkie talkie in one hand, a black vest strapped to his chest, and pistol hanging off his hip.

"Mrs. Allen. Boys."

"Did they find him?" Mom asked.

"Find who?" Larry asked, latching onto Mom's leg.

"Hush now, Larry."

"He's still missing, Ma'am. The warden wanted me to stop by and tell you that all homes are on lockdown for the night. We've got guards posted throughout the housing, so there's no reason to worry. We're pretty sure he left the reservation."

I remembered hearing the story of an inmate who'd gone missing in Massachusetts. That was before I was born. Dad said the guy had hidden in the coat closet of the warden's house before they brought in the dogs and found him days later. No harm to anyone except his dehydrated self. I made a mental note to check the closet before bed that night.

"You'll be fine, Mrs. Allen." He must've seen the concern on her face as I did. "But I could have someone posted in the house if you'd like."

Mom composed herself at that. "Nonsense. We'll be fine. Right, kids?"

"Yeah, we'll be fine, Denny," I said.

Denny shook my hand and then Larry's.

"I knew you men would be up to the challenge. Now," he reached his hands into a side pocket and produced two Snickers bars, "your Dad said I should give these to your Mom, in case you men ended up being a big help tonight."

"Oooo me, me! I'm a big help," Larry said.

"I'm sure you are, Larry." He looked to Mom, and she nodded.

I was not above bribery. If Dad thought giving us candy bars would help us stay calm, I wasn't about to protest the ethical structure of the deal. Full candy bars were as rare as Christmas Day in the Allen household.

After further assurance that all would be well, Denny hoisted Larry up over his head, flying him like a plane. Then he left with a smiling farewell.

"I like Denny," Larry said, his mouth gummed with nougat.

I watched the kid dance away in joyful ignorance. Until bedtime, Mom and I tried to ignore the rumble of guard trucks and the odd sounds coming from the prison. We were allowed to turn the television volume up high that night. She sat up with us, knitting a blanket for a friend, always with one eye on the door.

CHAPTER TWENTY-TWO

M orning came, and we were still on lockdown. Not such a bad thing. Mom let us eat as much cereal as we wanted, and then the morning was all television.

But remember, something had happened to my brain. Up until the day of my whooping in the greenhouse, I'd been oblivious to the evils of the world. Oh, I knew there was bad stuff out there. However, there was always a part of me that knew I was safe. Evil had not found its way into the things I loved. So, I could eat my cereal and watch my cartoons. Deep inside, I knew that if there was any real threat, I wouldn't be doing any of those things.

But then came the betrayal. Suddenly, evil was not only out there, but capable of seeping in through the vents in whatever cozy little place we'd ever call home.

Although I enjoyed my morning, I needed an answer just as much as I knew Mom did.

It finally came.

Dad came home, and I heard whispered words coming from the kitchen. Then he left with a mug of coffee in his hand, a nod of his head, and a curt, "Boys." I instantly started to feel better because if there was something *really* wrong, Dad would tell us. It was as simple as that. Warden Allen protected his sons, though not at the expense of the truth.

The official call came before lunch—*All Clear*. By then, Mom had gotten used to the situation. The noon whistle blew, and Larry and I ran outside to play, lunchboxes in hand.

We devoured sandwiches while dangling our feet in the creek. We sat there digesting and trying to skip stones across the lazy water. When we grew bored of that, we declared total war on the British.

Larry and I came home sweaty and smiling at the second whistle. When we arrived, there were three prison trucks and a couple of sedans parked in the front of the house. Mom was sitting on the front porch knitting. She looked up when we appeared.

"Who's here?" I asked.

She stood from the rocking chair.

"Your father and some of the others." She set the knitting down on the chair and stretched. "I need to pick some things up at the store. Why don't you quietly use the bathroom and then we'll go?"

"Argh, Mom, can we stay?"

"Yeah, stay!" Larry repeated.

"I'll let you pick out snacks," Mom said.

"Snacks!" Larry said. "I want some snacks!"

My sidekick was easily susceptible to outside enticements. I, on the other hand, had no such vice. Still, it didn't matter. We were up against a formidable foe.

"Then it's settled," said Mom, firing the salvo that ended the battle. "Get cleaned up and we'll go."

The mind that had unearthed every redcoat hiding in a one-mile radius now hatched a plan for the ages.

"Hey, Mom?"

She looked up from brushing the dust from Larry's backside.

"I'm pretty tired. I didn't sleep well last night. You know, because of the—" I threw a glance at the prison.

Total lie. I'd slept like the dead. In fact, my slumber had been better than good. I'd caught the lost prisoner in my dreams.

Mom's eyes narrowed and I tried to make my face look as tired as I could.

"Fine," she said.

Victory, thy name is James Allen.

"But you stay in your room and leave your father and the others alone."

"I promise." I was sincere. All I really wanted to do was kick back and enjoy some blessed air conditioning, maybe map out my next attack against the British.

Mom and Larry left, and I cleaned up in the bathroom.

When I emerged, I heard Dad's laugh. It wasn't something we heard often. Hell, we rarely heard him laugh. That got me curious: *spy time.* Every good general knows he has to play that role when needed.

A loud, "Ohhhhhhh!" erupted from the living room as I approached. I froze.

"Now watch this!" someone said. Then another, "Ohhhhhh!"

I moved closer. When I got to the living room and peeked in, the first thing I noted was Dad standing with a huge grin, a clear glass in his hand with some dark liquid in it.

"Ohhhhhhh!" went the group again. Dad chuckled.

That's when I realized they were all staring at the television.

"Wait, wait. Here's the best part," one of the assistant wardens said. He had the VCR remote in his hand. Then, "Ohhhhhh!" from the group.

What were they watching?

I snuck around to get a better view. The men were glued forward and didn't notice me shifting behind them.

There were beer bottles all over the coffee table plus a drink in each man's hand. Some held clear glasses filled with an amber liquid like Dad.

"Who wants to see it again?" the assistant warden asked. He did something with the remote, pressed play and then, "Ohhhhhhh!" erupted again.

Now I was curious. What in the world would elicit this reaction from men who daily dealt with hardened criminals?

I'd made it to a position where I could see now. It wasn't easy because everyone in attendance crowded close for a view of the television, but I caught a lucky sliver of air.

"Here we go again," said the man holding the remote.

I couldn't at first make out what I was watching. I could see some industrial facility. There was a large metal container looking thing on the screen. Then the bin shifted left, and I saw what it contained. Trash. Just trash. Yet the room erupted again anyway. "Ohhhhh!"

I was so confused that I took a couple of steps forward. What was I missing, and why were they so happy and laughing? The beer and the liquor had to mean something. Dad never drank more than a little brandy. I'd never seen him drunk. I was pretty sure he was now. Hell, they all were.

The tape rewound, and I watched intently. The trash bin was in its original position, then it moved, like before. The first hint of the trash came into view.

"Here he is. Good 'ol Ivy Hodge." The room erupted in fresh laughter.

Who was Ivy Hodge?

I took another step forward. I could touch the man in the back row if I'd wanted.

The tape went back again. These guys were getting a kick

out of this strange video. I thought that maybe it was an inside joke, something only adults understood. I'd been at the butt end of a raunchy joke before that I didn't understand. I'd laugh and try to change the subject.

"Okay, last time," the man with the remote said.

I strained to see. The bin. The moving. The trash.

Then I saw it. No, not it. *Them*. I saw them interspersed with the debris inside the bin. There, serving as a hilarity for everyone in the room, was a collection of body parts, two arms, a leg, and a head that looked like an old squished pumpkin.

I ran to my room, terrified of something I couldn't name.

CHAPTER TWENTY-THREE

I had dreams that night. Dreams of drifting body parts floating through the ether. I didn't know this Ivy Hodge, but I would forever remember him in the only way that I'd seen him: as scattered bits of trash left for someone else to clean up.

Morning came along with the full story. I scooped my cereal carefully as Dad recounted Ivy Hodge's tale.

"Someone locked him into the trash bin. We'll probably never find out who, but that doesn't matter. I've never had an escape on my watch, and I still don't."

"Honey, I don't think you should be talking about this with the kids at breakfast."

"This is life, Esther," he said dismissively, then turned to Larry. "Tell me, what happens when you do something bad?"

Larry thought on that for a moment. "I get in trouble."

"Good. Now, what happens when you take a big chance and do something dangerous?"

Larry thought again. "I could get hurt?"

Dad beamed at Mom. "See? They understand."

Mom shook her head.

"Why did he try to escape?" I asked.

Dad shrugged and dug into his grapefruit. "We'll probably never know. Some get bored. Others have something they want on the outside. Who's to say?"

"Are they unhappy in prison?"

Dad looked at me in a way I'd never seen. He sucked his teeth for a moment. "When people do wrong, sometimes they don't know how they can go about making that thing right again. That's where we come in. We give them the chance to make things right by serving their time, doing their number. They don't enjoy it, but they have to do it. Do you understand? We try to make it comfortable for them because they're human beings, but human beings aren't happy being cooped up all the time. And so, like birds . . ." He made a gesture with his hand of something taking off.

I thought about this for a moment.

"How did he die?"

"Dean," Mom said. The warning was clear.

Again, Dad ignored her. "As far as we can tell, Mr. Hodge had an accomplice who helped him hide in that compactor. He didn't get out of the bin in time because he didn't factor on someone coming by and turning it on. That's all. It was all part of a daily routine. So, the compactor got him. Just plain old bad luck."

I filed away dying in a trash bin as probably the worst way to die.

Dad gulped down the last dregs of coffee and stood, a man reborn. "You all have a wonderful day."

He walked over and planted a wet kiss on Mom's cheek and then actually took the time to tousle our hair, one head in each hand. Larry loved it. To me, it was a thousand spiders crawling on my head.

When Dad was gone, my mother exhaled and attacked

the dishes with less finesse than usual. I brought my bowl to the sink. "I can do the dishes, Mom."

Mom was muttering to herself.

"Mom, are you okay?"

She looked at me, fire in her eyes. I took a careful step back, a bowl still in hand. Then she said something I'll never forget.

"James, learn from your father. Don't be like him. Learn from him. If you're confused about that, ask me about it some other time."

CHAPTER TWENTY-FOUR

With Dad's perfect record still intact, the Allen family settled into Virginia life. I'm not sure if Mom had anything to do with it, but every night Dad would come home and take me out to the shed where we'd tinker with the four-wheeler. The parts were there along with sketched instructions left by Carlisle.

"Good man, that Carlisle," Dad would say if we encountered a particularly difficult fix that he wouldn't have been able to do without help.

We got in a routine. Morning breakfast. Fighting the Revolution in the fields. Whistle, lunch. Nap for Larry and quiet time for yours truly. Then more playtime outside.

To summarize, I was in heaven—pure, unadulterated bliss.

I should've known it would all go to crap.

LARRY WAS ONCE AGAIN PLAYING the role of a spy. I had to admit he was getting good. I told him so. That for sure, got him going.

We were snooping on the neighbors in a gray, warm drizzle when it really started pissing down on us.

"We should probably go home," I said, swiping a sheet of water from my face.

"Nooooo," Larry whined. "Please, Jimmy. Let's play."

He danced around in the rain like Gene Kelly. I laughed at the face he was making, a cross between a clown and a kid with a severe spinal injury.

"Okay." I grabbed his hands, and we spun around and around. I tilted my face up to the sky. Big fat raindrops hit every inch.

"Faster!" Larry screamed with a giggle on his lips.

"Here we go." I opened my eyes to make sure we weren't about to go whirling into a tree. There *he* was. Standing in the rain. Just staring. Brady Bruce.

The shock of it made me loosen the hold I had on Larry. He flew away laughing as he splashed into the mud. I went for my brother, concerned that I might've hurt him again.

"Do it again!" he said.

I looked up to see Brady Bruce. He was gone. Vanished.

How had he disappeared so quickly? Maybe it was my imagination; I told you, I have an active one.

"Come on, Larry. It's time to go home."

Larry complained only a little. We walked home hand in hand. Thinking back, I wish I could have that moment again —two brothers at peace. Time would eventually stomp on that beautiful memory.

A word to the wise from your humble servant Jimmy Allen: Gather ye rosebuds, folks, and remember what they smell like when you do. They tend to rot pretty fast.

We were rounding the last turn to home when a voice cracked through the rain.

"Looked like you boys were having fun."

I turned slowly. Brady Bruce was walking along in the

rain, swinging his nightstick like it was the freest form of exercise he could get.

"We're going home," I said quickly.

After all, he was fast. Faster than I'd put on the big man. He cut in front of us. There was nothing to do but stop.

"Which one of you is Larry?" he asked. I knew he knew. He asked the question in one of those voices meant for a kid six and under.

"Me. I'm Larry," my brother said, even raising his hand in the air.

"Ah. That's right. You're the strong one."

Bruce looked at me, and I felt cold all over. My grip on Larry's hand tightened.

"Owwwww. That hurts!"

I ignored his complaint. "Come on, Larry. Mom needs us at home."

I tried to get around the hulking guard, but he shifted to block us.

"Your mom's not home," Bruce said. Something in his voice. "She said I should look out for you two lunkheads."

That's when we met eyes. I mustered every ounce of Dad's bravery, every drop of General Washington's courage, but I still wanted to wither away.

We stood there in a standoff.

"*Everything okay?*" came a voice.

It was from Carlisle. I could have kissed him.

Brady Bruce turned around, swinging his club into his hand. "What the hell are you doing out here?"

"Checking for rain spout leaks, Boss," Carlisle said, pointed to the closest house. "Jimmy. Larry. How you boys doin'?"

My God, my body flooded with relief. It was short-lived, though.

"Get back to the prison," Bruce ordered.

Carlisle mulled that over for a moment. He was wearing a homemade poncho that looked like it'd seen service in the Civil War.

"I sure need to get this work done, Boss. Last year one of the gutters got knocked off in heavy rain and almost fell on someone."

"Well, we wouldn't want that now, would we?" Bruce said with a sneer.

"No, Boss."

Bruce's eyes came back to me.

"Come on, kids. I'll take you home."

"Why don't you let me take them, Boss? I'm sure you've got more important things to do."

Holy Carlisle, blessed Carlisle.

Bruce's body flexed, and he stepped over to the older man. The club came up and tapped him in the middle of the chest. "Why don't you mind your own fucking business, inmate?"

"Yes, Boss. Just minding my own business. Warden and Mrs. Allen told me to keep my eyes out for the boys. Isn't that right, Jimmy?"

"Yes, that's right," I said, too quickly.

Bruce's eyes flicked between Carlisle and the Allen boys. Then the club tipped up forty-five degrees and nudged Carlisle's chin up.

"I've got my eye on you, boy."

Carlisle didn't move a muscle. I wished he'd snatch the weapon from Bruce's hand and serve it to him for lunch.

The walkie talkie on Bruce's hip squawked. *Bruce, need you at the front gate. New prisoners to process.*

The stick came down, and he answered the call.

"I'll be right there." He straightened his rain-soaked uniform and stared down Carlisle one last time. "Fresh meat, my favorite." He tapped Carlisle on each shoulder with his club, like a king knighting a lord. Then, he walked away.

When he was out of sight, Carlisle ushered us to the greenhouse. I was shivering uncontrollably by then. Even Larry noticed, and he wrapped his little arm around me.

"Larry, there's a stack of clean towels in my office. Do you mind grabbing them and bringing them out?"

"Yes, Sir."

Larry marched off, and I sat on the edge of one of the many raised beds. When my brother was out of earshot, Carlisle asked, "Are you okay, Jimmy?"

"Yeah."

"Good. Cuz that there's an evil man."

I looked up at him, not the least bit embarrassed when tears came to my eyes. "He scares me."

Carlisle nodded. "That means you're a good soul. And you know what? He scares me too, Jimmy."

"Really?"

"Really."

"Why does he scare you? You're as big as him."

He reached over and fiddled with one of the leaves on a tomato plant.

"You spend enough time behind bars, and you get to know the look of a man. You ever heard of a snap judgment?"

"I think so." I didn't want to admit that I didn't know.

"Well, it means that you pretty much know what a man's like seconds after you meet him. Has that ever happened to you?"

"Yes! With Brady Bruce."

Carlisle nodded appreciatively. "I thought so. You got the gift, Jimmy."

My tears were gone now.

"What gift?"

Carlisle sat down beside me.

"There's a lot of good in this world. A lot of bad too. The trick is to go towards one while running like a banshee away from the other. At least that's what my grandma used to say to me."

"But you're in jail."

The words came out of my mouth before I could catch them and slam them back down my gullet. I remembered what Dad had told me about talking to inmates about what they'd done on the outside and about how they were doing their time like honorable men.

"Yup. Cuz I did some bad things before I came here. Hell, I did bad things since I've been in here." He looked down the length of the greenhouse for Larry. Satisfied, he shifted back to me. "But deep down, I am a good man. Always have been. You understand that?"

"Sure." There were plenty of superheroes with tainted pasts. "Why are you in jail, Carlisle?" Again, with the runaway words. Good move, Jimmy. "Never mind, you don't have to tell me."

He looked again for Larry. No Larry. He probably became distracted by Carlisle's knick-knacks.

"It's okay. You don't need to know. I'm not proud of what I've done. All the same, I can't change it. I did some things on the outside that I still need to atone for. Do you understand what 'atone' means?"

"No."

"I guess the easiest way to say it is that it means to put things right. You understand? That's why I'm doing my number and not complaining about it. Don't get me wrong; I was angry for a long time. But you see, I was angry at me. I hurt a lot of people. Hurt my family." He stared down at his hands. "Can you believe that I learned how to be a good man on the inside?"

Dad would've liked to hear that.

Larry showed up with the towels. "Here, Jimmy."

"Thanks," I said.

We dried off a bit and waited for the rain to slacken. We talked with Carlisle about plants and flowers. The soil has to be good, he said, over and over again. Gotta have good soil. It wasn't until I started writing this that I finally figured out what he meant.

However, when I got home, all I could think about was what Carlisle had said about the world being full up with good and bad.

I wondered which side I might end upon.

CHAPTER TWENTY-FIVE

Sometimes I'd see Brady Bruce at the front gate or driving past in the prison pickup. He'd always stare at me. Always. I didn't like it. I thought about telling Dad, but I didn't. I can't explain why. Maybe I didn't want to admit to the warden that there were things in life that were starting to get the better of me.

Summer went on. Dad and I got the four-wheeler working with Carlisle's help. It got to the point where even Carlisle's detailed notes couldn't help, so Dad asked him to do the work. Thank goodness. With Carlisle at the helm, Marauder was up and running in two days.

"She could use a polish here and there, but as far as I can see, she's ready for combat," Carlisle announced.

It was done and I had free reign with the growling beast.

"Make sure you bring it back to Carlisle when you're finished riding," said Dad. "Help him get it cleaned up. Whatever he says."

"Yes, sir," I said, ready to give away a kidney for the chance at roving freedom. I'd never met a kid my age who had a four-wheeler. And here I was, Jimmy Allen, about to ravage the countryside with my very own.

"Make sure Larry stays off. You got that?"

No problem with that. "Yes, *sir*," I said.

Dad gave me a pat on the back and told me I could start it up. "She's all yours, son."

I had never heard my father speak such sweet-sounding words.

I rotated the key, and the engine came to life with a sputter and stayed alive with a healthy growl.

"That noise should run itself out in a day," Carlisle said. "Made some adjustments this morning."

To me, it was music. I revved the engine, feet and hands ready to go to work.

I spent the day roaming the fields, helmetless and free, splashing through the lowest points of the creek and relishing the power beneath my butt. I wondered if this was what Washington felt while riding his faithful horse, Blueskin. Power isn't showing force. Power is having the *choice* to do so if one wishes.

I waved to the patrol and felt the thrill as I rumbled past them. Some of the guards egged me on, whooping as I shot forward. But even helming this mighty machine, I was careful not to approach any vehicles driven or occupied by Brady Bruce.

In the days to come, *everyone* knew I had a four-wheeler. When asked, I would brag about building it from scratch. It wasn't really a lie. More than once, I'd scratched myself while helping Carlisle.

My ego inflated to canyon size and lifted me to the heavens on my four-wheeled harbinger of terror.

Falling back to Earth was a bitch.

CHAPTER TWENTY-SIX

We'd gotten back from a tour of my new school.

"How was it?" Mom asked.

"It smells like old chalk and mildew," I said.

She cocked her head at me. "Is that a proper thing to say?"

"It's the truth."

"What is that?" asked Larry.

"James, you should learn to hold your tongue sometimes."

"What's 'mildew'?" Larry pressed.

"It's a bunch of dirty spores that go in through your nose and slither up to your brain. If the doctors don't get to them in time, they—"

"James! Don't scare your brother."

Larry's eyes were wide, but he wasn't scared. I put my finger to my lips, and he got the drill. I would continue the tale of the brain-eating mildew later.

"Mom, do I have to go to school?" I asked, refocusing on the road ahead.

"Of course you do."

"Why?"

"Are you sure you want me to answer that question?"

"I know. Because if we don't go, we'll be dumb, right?"

Mom's face turned momentarily to look at me. She tried to seem shocked, but I saw the smile tugging at the corners of her mouth. "Who told you that?"

I shrugged.

"Well, I don't think that's appropriate."

"Did *you* always love school, Mom?" I asked. I'd seen the gap in her armor. What kid wouldn't dive in?

"Not always."

"See?"

"You don't have to love it all the time."

"All the same, you say we should do things that we love. Like Dad and prisons."

She thought on that for a long moment, maybe a couple of miles on the road. Mom was careful with her words now. She knew my game.

"That's true. You should do what you love."

"Do you love being a parent?"

I assumed the answer would come right out. Mom was one of those mothers, I thought. But she paused. The pause went on for much longer than I liked. I started to feel an itch on my neck.

The words then came out as if she'd rehearsed them. "Of course I do. Of course. I love my children."

Regardless, that wasn't what I'd asked. I'd asked my mom if she loved *being a parent*—a small difference, perhaps, but a difference nonetheless.

"Here we are," Mom said as we pulled up to the house. "Boys, help with the bags, will you?"

CHAPTER TWENTY-SEVEN

I left Larry to his nap and went to find my four-wheeler, which I tucked into a dry spot next to the greenhouse. I could see upon my approach that Carlisle had wiped it down as he did every morning whether I'd ridden it or not.

I was about to knock on the greenhouse door when I heard talking.

I knew that voice.

I put my ear to the door. All I could hear were broken muffles.

"Ever . . . and your friends . . . be in . . ."

I eased the door open a crack, careful not to let it squeak. As soon as the humid air hit me, I knew the voice belonged to Brady Bruce. My flight response told me to run home. I wanted nothing to do with the man.

I heard Carlisle say, "Yes, Boss."

I couldn't leave Carlisle alone with that man, no matter the consequences. But what could I do? I was only a kid, and Brady Bruce was a gimlet-eyed freak-a-zoid who could grind me into the ground like a cigarette butt.

I took a deep breath and went left, skirting the plants

that effortlessly concealed my approach. Tomatoes. Green beans. Squash. I ignored every one of them. My focus was dead ahead.

"You tell me what you've got going with the Allen family," demanded Bruce.

"I don't know what you mean, Boss."

I was careful to step around a pile of debris we'd clipped from the plants the day before.

"You know what I mean. You've got a meal ticket, and I want it."

"I swear, Boss. Nothing's going on."

I could see them now; Carlisle was standing with his hat in his hands. Brady Bruce had his stick out. That damned stick. Just the sight of it gave me nightmares.

"You are a lying son of a bitch," Bruce said, poking Carlisle in the chest with the thing. "I heard about your little four-wheeler project. You telling me you didn't get nothing out of that?"

"Nothing, Boss. I swear."

Carlisle wasn't cowering. I admired that.

Quick as a whip, the nightstick swung and hit Carlisle in the meaty part of his upper arm. Carlisle's face flinched, but other than that, he didn't move. Then the stick came from the left and hit him on the other side. Carlisle still didn't move.

But I did.

"I saw that!" I said, rushing in, not sure what power was moving my legs. My insides felt like jelly, and my stomach was about to heave. My words weren't mine but came up from some primal place within my troubled little soul. "You touch him one more time, and I'll tell my dad!"

Bruce's face registered surprise. That surprise turned into his supplicating smile, the one that made me want to puke and run. And not necessarily in that order.

"Well if it isn't our little sport. How ya' doing, kid?"

"My name's Jimmy. If you don't leave right now . . ."

He threw his head back and laughed. "What? You're gonna tell your daddy on me?" He held up his arms; the nightstick still clutched in his meaty fist. "Don't hurt me, mister! I give up!"

He laughed again.

The words stuck in my mouth. The guard was so big and seemed to be getting bigger with every second. By the time Carlisle spoke, I could have sworn Brady Bruce was as tall as a mountain.

"Why don't you let me take him home, Boss?"

Bruce thought about that. He thought about that long and hard.

"You two better stay out of my way, you hear me?"

"Yes, Boss," Carlisle said.

"And you?" Bruce said, pointing his nightstick at my face. "You need to stay out of trouble. I don't want to have to report you to your daddy. He's a good man and doesn't need to be worrying about you getting into trouble with the inmates."

All I could do was nod feebly.

Bruce laughed.

The nightstick swung, sweeping every item taller than a sheet of paper off Carlisle's desk. "*Tch, tch, tch.* Clean this shit up, boy, before I write you up for being a slob."

He winked at me, and then he was gone, swinging his stick at his side.

"You okay?" Carlisle asked when the bully was gone.

I nodded, however, I felt anything but okay.

"I hate him," I said. I knew I didn't need to say it.

"Every man gets his due in the end."

"Why does he act like that?"

Carlisle looked at the mess on the floor and bit his lip.

"You know, some men got so much hate inside them, and for no one but themselves. The hate gets so bad that they need to lash out at others before it builds up to the point where it chokes them to death."

"So, you're saying I should feel sorry for Brady Bruce?"

Carlisle chuckled warmly. "We all got choices to make about what we do with our feelings. I'd say every man in this prison, including Boss Bruce there, made the wrong choice at one point or another in that regard. The difference is, folks doing their number in here are trying to make it right. Dunno if I can say the same for Boss Bruce."

He knelt and began picking his belongings up off the floor. I stooped down to help him.

"Nah, don't do that. The boss told me to do it. I don't want you getting in any more trouble."

Reluctantly, I stood, my hands jittery at my sides.

Carlisle looked up at me. "Don't look so upset."

Mortification ran all over me. I'd hoped it wasn't showing that I wanted to cry.

He looked back down at his stuff and repeated, "Yep. Every man gets his due."

CHAPTER TWENTY-EIGHT

"Jimmy! Jimmy!" Larry's voice shocked me awake. It was 5:38 am. When I finally realized what he was yelling about; I had to bury my hands underneath my pillow to avoid smacking him.

There was no way around it. School was finally upon me like a boulder racing downhill.

I was going into the fifth grade, and I'd been to a total of five schools in five years. I approached it like an aged coal miner stepping into the metal elevator for the thousandth time.

"Aren't you excited, James? A new school!" Mom said she inspected my backpack to make sure I had everything. She straightened the collar of my shirt. I tried to wriggle free.

"Look at me," she said, and there was sadness in her eyes. I didn't get it. I wasn't being shipped off to battle. In eight hours, I'd be back in this very spot, and she'd be praying for a single, sacred moment of peace and quiet.

"I wanna go on the bus!" Larry said.

Mom laughed. The sadness was gone temporarily. "Are you excited about seeing the bus?"

"Yes!" He jumped up and down like his underwear was made of hamsters. He continued to chatter away as Mom walked us down the drive, past the gate, and onto the main road that came from town out to the prison.

"Am I the first stop?" I asked.

"Yes."

I exhaled sharply. The anxiety had finally hit, as it always did at this very moment. After all, a new school was a new school. There would be the humiliating introduction of yours truly to the class. A hundred eyes would be boring into me like hand drills. There would be the equally embarrassing task of finding someone to sit next to at lunch. Class was easy. Teachers always assigned seats. Not lunch. As far as my new schoolmates were concerned, I might as well be a leper. Or worse, a communist.

"I'm so excited for you, James," Mom said. I could hear the waterworks coming. I decided to throw her a lifeline.

"I'll be fine, Mom. I promise."

That seemed to make it worse. There was no pleasing this woman.

Larry ran around Mom and grabbed my hand. The strange thing was that I needed that more than I realized. Something about his touch gave me the courage for the day. Nothing gives your life meaning like the simple fact of being needed, no matter how trivial the moment.

"Don't you look," Mom searched for the word, "handsome. I wish I'd brought the camera."

God, *handsome*. If words could wound—

Not to mention the thought of a picture. I never understood parents taking photographs on the first day of school. Didn't they know we were nervous enough? I didn't need the awkward pose, the gushing, and all that so that she could stare at a permanent record of my anxiety.

A large engine started as a mumble in the distance then

grew to a roar, and here was the bus, farting out enough exhaust to destroy an ecosystem. I saw the white hair of the driver. The bus was empty. First on and last off as always—the longest ride by a mile. Lucky prison kid.

As the bus braked to a squealing stop, Mom bent down to give me one last hug.

"Thank you, James, for being such a young man about this."

"You're welcome," I said, not knowing what else to say to that. Truth be told, at that moment, all I wanted to do was rush into her arms and have her tell me everything would be okay. But I didn't. I gave her a stoic response and ushered my thumping heart onto the bus.

CHAPTER TWENTY-NINE

The James Allen Report on Patrick Henry Elementary School, Slater, Virginia:

Playground: First-rate. One of those metal tube-slides that could give you a concussion and tetanus simultaneously. Perfect. Swings, fine, but for girls. A short slope on one side of the field adjoining the blacktop. Great for tumbling.

The gym: Smells like sweat and Comet. The climbing rope looks like it couldn't hold a sweater button, let alone a medium-sized ten-year-old.

The teachers: A proper mix of young and old. The young ones overly sweet, the old ones patient, but with permanent scowls.

The lunchroom: Smells like sweat and Comet.

Lunch itself wasn't as bad as I'd thought it would be. The kids were nice, and two others were new to the school: a boy and a girl. The boy was a little nerdy for my taste and skinny enough for his cheekbones to show, but he was okay. His name was Kenji, and he was half-Japanese. I knew because I asked him. It was okay back then.

We didn't hear words like diversity, and yet none of us

blinked at having kids of every color in class. They were just kids. If they were cool, that was a plus. It wasn't until we were all older that the lines of separation were drawn.

I'm still not sure why we bother to recognize how different everyone is so that we can say we're all equal.

Kenji's father worked for a car company and his mom stayed at home, though she spent most days with her Japanese friends. He was an only child and spent his days reading books. Lots and lots of books.

"You'd like this one, Jimmy," he said one day, pulling a book from his zipper-bulging bag. He carried it everywhere even after our teacher said he could leave it with the rest of the book bags.

"What is it?"

He looked left and right, like he was about to tell me the combination of Fort Knox.

"Have you ever played Dungeons and Dragons?"

An excited shiver tingled down my back. "No," I whispered. "What's that?"

He showed me the cover of the book. It said Monster Manual on the front and had a spine-chilling picture of some multi-tentacled beast.

"I'm building a troop and I need warriors." He looked around again. "Well, not just warriors. Magic users. Thieves. Assassins."

This kid spoke my language.

"I like George Washington," I said. I don't know why I said it. I never told any other kids what I imagined when I played by myself.

Kenji didn't laugh. He didn't look at me with even one bugged-out eye; instead, he nodded sagely.

"Then you're exactly who I've been looking for."

From that point on, Kenji and I were inseparable at school. I had a new Tour of Duty coming.

CHAPTER THIRTY

Kenji seemed to have an endless supply of books and an equally generous capacity to lend them to me. They were well cared for. His babies. He said his parents bought him any books he wanted because they weren't around much. That sounded like heaven to me.

It took a couple of days for me to figure out the basics of this Dungeons and Dragons game. Kenji was the self-proclaimed Dungeon Master. That was fine with me because he knew the rules. And boy did he have an imagination. He was the smartest kid in class and the best storyteller. I wondered why I was the only one who noticed the latter. To the rest of the class, he was this twittery little kid who shook when he had to get up to answer a question. But to me, he'd tell stories that had my toes tingling with excitement and suspense.

As Dungeon Master, Kenji was in charge of devising the adventures and running the game. It was a big job. There were notes to take, maps to coordinate, characters to keep track of, and treasure to divvy out. There were tons of different character types to choose from. I decided to become a ranger, mainly because Kenji said they were good with nature, sometimes had an animal companion, and were good with bows. Secretly I wanted to be an assassin, but I didn't tell Kenji. Assassins were evil characters, and my new friend was squarely on the side of the good. His role was a Paladin, basically a super knight, and there were no more altruistic characters than Paladins. A Paladin and an assassin wouldn't have gotten along. At least that was my opinion, and I did not want to offend my new friend.

"The bottom of the tree you're hiding in turns to fire," Kenji said as we wound our way through some dank forest in search of a humungous cache of gold guarded by a minor demon. In reality, we were sitting at the end of our lunch table, whispering back and forth, our character sheets in front of us, divided by an open folder Kenji called a "module," whose contents only he, as Dungeon Master, could see. Presumably, it was a map of the forest and other things only a Dungeon Master could understand, like tables and probability sheets that predicted outcomes based on throws of dice. I cared nothing about those. My tree was on fire.

"The mage in the black cloak laughs as the fire licks its way up to your feet," Kenji said.

"I'll shoot him with my bow," I said, my heart thumping.

Kenji handed me a twenty-sided die. "From where you're sitting and the angle and the branches, you have to roll a seventeen or above to hit him."

"Ahh. Come on."

Kenji sat stone-faced, boring into me, ignoring the unfinished Wonder Bread and salami sandwich next to the open folder.

"Okay. I'll take the shot." I gripped the die in my hand and blew on it for luck. "Wait. Can I still get away?"

Kenji smiled. "You can."

He was good at these little twists. The frontal assault was

rarely the right path with him as Dungeon Master. He rewarded cunning, diplomacy, and kindness.

"Okay. I'm gonna jump to the next tree and flee to fight another day."

I tried to say it as he did, all grand like something out of Shakespeare. It sounded more like Shel Silverstein.

Kenji looked down at his notes.

"You make the jump in time. Fire covers the spot you just left. You make your way from one tree to the next, your dexterity obvious as you leap like a spider monkey." I laughed at that, imagining myself diving and snatching branches as I went. "You've made it to—"

The school bell rang, marking the end of the lunch period. Kenji closed the module with the solemnity of a priest ending a Gospel reading. "To be continued."

"Come on, Kenji. What happens next?"

He grinned. "A Dungeon Master never skips ahead."

I groaned and shook my head. "Come on." I grabbed his brown lunch bag to take to the trash.

"I can take that," he said.

"It's the least I can do. You make me want to come to school."

It was one of those off the cuff things you say. I didn't think about it because it was true.

Kenji's mouth spread in the most genuine smile I'd seen.

"Then my job here is complete," he said with a bow.

I rolled my eyes and couldn't help laughing. "Come on, oh, high Dungeon Master."

I fixed him in a headlock and dragged him over to the trashcan. Kids were staring at the spectacle, and I didn't care. Let them laugh. I'd avoided being roasted by an evil wizard.

CHAPTER THIRTY-ONE

"Can I have a friend over?"

Mom stopped the vegetable chopping and looked at me. "You have a friend?"

Here we go.

"Yes, without a doubt, I have a friend."

I obviously understood what she was thinking. No parent wants their kid visiting a prison. I'd never had a friend over.

"What's his name?"

"Kenji."

"That's an interesting name. Is he a nice boy?"

"Mom!"

"Sorry. Of course, you can have your friend over. Would you like me to call his mother?"

"She doesn't speak English."

I didn't know if that was the truth, but the lie had slipped out like a sneeze.

"Then, his father?"

"All we need is a note for the bus."

Mom slid the onion she had chopped into a pan. The pieces hit with a stinging hiss.

"Fine with me."

"Thanks!"

I had Kenji's phone number written on the back of my hand. I slipped to my parents' bedroom for privacy and dialed his house.

"Jimmy?"

"Yeah, it's me."

"What did your mom say?"

"She said you could come over."

"Awesome. Want me to bring figurines?"

He'd told me about the little metal D&D figurines he painted and sometimes used for games.

"Sure." I tried not to sound overly excited. Keep it cool. In truth, I was buzzing with adrenaline. My first friend over *and* figurines? I could barely keep from vibrating out of my socks.

"Great, he said. "I'll see you at school tomorrow?"

"Wait. Kenji?"

"Yeah?"

"What happens with the wizard?"

"You wanna play it out *now*?"

"Can we?" I said weakly. I felt weird. The way he answered, I almost felt ashamed. But his role as Dungeon Master had elevated him to adult status in my eyes.

"By all means. Sure." He took a moment, then I heard papers rustling. "Okay, you slip off the last tree. The wizard's yelling something you can't hear. Wait. It's a spell. The air around you tingles."

"Run! I want to run!" I said as loud as I dared.

"You try to run, but your legs are stuck in place. The wizard has frozen you on the spot, and he's coming your way. He's laughing again. High and loud like a hyena."

"Jeez, Kenji. What the hell am I gonna do now?"

"Just as your heart feels like it's going to explode out of

your chest, an arrow zips past your head. Then another. The wizard screams, and suddenly, your legs can move again. The spell is disrupted."

"What? Who—"

"Someone calls your name. You look that way and see a shock of blonde hair waving in the wind; the figure is wearing leather armor that fits her bodacious form perfectly."

"Bodaci—? What does—wait . . . it's a girl?"

"Not just a girl. A female ranger. She wants you to come with her."

With no other choice, I assented. "Fine. I'll go with her."

Great. The last thing I'd expected was to be saved by a girl.

"To be continued," Kenji said. I thought I heard mirth in his voice.

"Alright, see you tomorrow, Kenji," I said, emasculated by *bodaciousness*.

CHAPTER THIRTY-TWO

Kenji wasn't at school the next day or the day after that. I called his house but no one answered. When Kenji did finally show up in class, his face was more drawn than it usually was, and his skin had this unnatural color like someone had squeezed all the juice out of it.

"Hey, Jimmy," Kenji said.

I could see that every syllable hurt him. "Are you okay?"

"I'm okay. Stomach bug." I think I backed away a half step before he added, "It's not contagious."

I relaxed at that. "Did you think up anything new?"

I didn't tell him I'd been dreaming about adventures. Wizards. Trolls. The odd dark elf creeping into my bedroom.

Kenji's old smile appeared. "I thought you'd never ask."

It took Kenji the rest of the week to look halfway decent again. Whenever I asked him if he needed help, he always shrugged it off. Our classmates treated him like more of a pariah than before. To them, he wasn't just a weirdo, he was some sort of diseased weirdo. That was fine with us. Everyone left us alone.

Well, almost everyone.

Did you ever meet a kid who was a bully magnet? Kenji was one of them. He'd take a good taunting equally from boys and girls. But while I balled my fists and imagined smashing their noses in, Kenji smiled and went back to whatever he was doing.

When I asked him about the bullying later, he'd murmur something about "Simpletons."

I didn't know what that word meant. I had to look it up. Once I knew the meaning of the word, I had to agree. Simpletons. In addition to that, they were also mean—out for a rise at the cost of someone else's sanity. I guess Kenji didn't want to admit that. I had no choice. I was no stranger to those types.

I remember it was a perfect fall day. The scorch of summer was finally letting off. Kenji and I were on the monkey bars. I could glide across like a gymnast. Kenji labored with each grip but took it in stride. Nobody would ever accuse Kenji of being a future Olympian unless the Olympics one day decided to introduce D&D campaigns as an event.

This particular day I think we were practicing crossing a river of lava. Kenji said the monkey bars were a rope bridge that we could only take from underneath. I was across in my usual simian time. Kenji struggled as I urged him on.

"Come on," I said. "The archers are right behind you."

Kenji's face strained. He was halfway across. He was going to make it.

Then a shadow passed across his body. A sixth-grade mouth-breather named Yancy pulled Kenji's pants down to his knees.

I was off the far step in a flash, running toward the interloper. The older kid was doubled over in laughter, pointing up at his victim. He'd not only gotten Kenji's corduroys, but he'd also managed to slip the underwear down as well.

"Hey, look at that!" said Yancy. "There's a Jap butt hanging in the air!"

Half of the class had noticed now. Yet for some reason, Kenji still hadn't dropped down. I was torn between watching the spectacle and wanting to throttle Yancy. He was maybe an inch taller than me. It was the gang of followers he had around him that made me stop.

"Kenji, get down," I said when the shock wore off, and my anger lowered down to med-high heat.

Kenji wouldn't get down. His pants were down around his ankles, and the teacher had noticed. Slowly and steadily. I don't think she knew what she was looking at.

"Kenji," I said. He looked down at me, terrified. Every kid in a mile's radius seemed to be laughing. "Drop down. It's okay."

He gave me a tiny nod and dropped down to the ground, writhing there, fumbling with his pants. It was like his hands didn't work. I pulled them up for him, underwear and all.

"Hey, look! Jap has a boyfriend!" Yancy called. "Why don't you kiss your boyfriend for helping you out, Jap boy. *Mushi-mushi,* kiss his *tushy!*"

My fist was flying before I knew what was happening. It careened straight for Yancy's head. I saw every detail of his face. The wide eyes. The parted lips. The nose waiting to be smashed.

The impact never came. Kenji pushed me away, and I stumbled to the ground.

That made everyone laugh even harder.

The teacher was there now.

"What in heavens is going on here? Yancy?"

"That kid's pants fell off while he was on the monkey bars. We were trying to help, but he wouldn't get down."

The teacher looked down at Kenji.

"Is that true?"

No hesitation from Kenji.

"Yes, Ma'am. I didn't have my belt on tight enough."

"What about you, Mr. Allen? Is there a reason you're on the ground?" She was either blind or stupid, and I didn't see a dog anywhere.

I couldn't say a word. I could only stare at my friend.

"I knocked him over by accident," Kenji said.

The teacher reached down to give me a hand up.

"I'm fine," I said, her touch was like a snail on my arm.

The school bell rang. "You boys and girls get inside. Go on now."

She left. Yancy and his gang didn't.

I was still on the ground when he approached. Yancy made like he was going to kick me in the side. I flinched to protect myself.

No kick came, but more laughs did.

"I'm so gonna kick your butt," Yancy said. Then to his peons, "Come on."

And then they were gone. Kenji knelt beside me.

"Are you okay?"

I looked back at him with incredulous eyes. "Me? What about you?"

"What about me?"

I scanned his face for any recognition of what'd just happened. Embarrassment. Mortification. Even regret. Nothing.

I got to my feet and brushed off my pants.

"I'm sorry, Jimmy."

Now I whirled on him. "You're sorry? Why don't you apologize to yourself? Half the school saw you naked!"

"It doesn't matter," he said.

I had no idea what he meant; his face was turning the color of cabernet.

"Yeah, you're right," I said. "It doesn't."

"Hey, do you want to come over this weekend? I drew up a new dungeon I thought you might like," Kenji said.

"No," I said, refusing to look at him as we headed back into the building. "We have plans."

I was too young to analyze it. But now, with hindsight eating away at my guts, I can tell you that right then and there I'd decided I could no longer be Kenji's friend.

My banishment of Kenji lasted a full weekend. What got me in touch with him again had nothing to do with remorse. What ten-year-old feels genuine remorse?

No. What got me to call my friend before school was none other than Brady Bruce.

CHAPTER THIRTY-THREE

I t was the Saturday after the pantsing episode at school. There was a new song on the radio. The DJ said it was "Pour Some Sugar on Me" by a group called Def Leppard. For some reason, the song had me entranced. I didn't know what they were singing about. To this day, I don't really listen to lyrics. It was more of the vibe of the song. This song made me feel alive. Something about the melodic insistence that the lead singer get sugar poured on him. Places I was used to, if you got sugar poured on you, it was only a matter of time before you were a hot mess and a walking ant trap.

Whatever it meant; I didn't care. This was my song.

I scanned radio stations the entire morning. Luckily the song was hitting the charts with a bang, and I listened to it a good ten times before Mom kicked me outside.

That was fine. I had the tune pressed in my brain. I hummed along as I made my way to the greenhouse. A ride on my four-wheeler would be a perfect accompaniment to my song-soaring mood.

"Who needs friends, anyway?" I asked the world.

Larry was back home, glued to cartoons. I was flying solo.

I rounded the last corner humming along, and there it was, my four-wheeler sitting on tires as flat as smooshed marshmallows.

Carlisle stepped out of the greenhouse. He didn't see me at first. He was too focused on the tools in his hands—a tire repair kit.

Then I noticed his swollen left eye.

He bent down to his task of fixing the first tire and I hung back. Something pulled me forward. I don't think it was altruism. I think it was curiosity.

"Hey Carlisle," I said, putting a dash of pep in my voice.

"Morning, Jimmy." He avoided my gaze.

Words stuck in my mouth. All the courage from a moment ago flew from my chest.

"I'm not sure you want to see this," he said, grabbing a cinder block and starting to make his jury-rigged jack system.

"What happened to my tires?"

"Don't worry," he said jovially, "I'll fix them."

"But what happened?"

"Ah, probably someone being cute."

Now the words came before I could clamp my teeth shut. "Was it Brady Bruce?"

Carlisle looked up at me. "Now why would you say that?"

Hmm, let's see. Because Bruce haunted my dreams? Because Bruce was the only person I could imagine doing such a thing? Or because I wanted it to be him?

"I don't know," I said honestly. "What happened to your eye?" I had to do something about my case of the blurts.

Carlisle put on a half-smile. "Ah, nothing for you to worry about."

I shifted from one foot to another while Carlisle got to work. It didn't take him long to get the first tire patched. He was on to the second before I had the guts to speak again.

"I thought we were friends."

He froze. Then he sat back on his knees and did this awkward scan left and right as if keeping an eye out for a guard. Then he turned to me.

"We *are* friends," he said, almost too quietly for me to hear.

"Then why can't you tell me what really happened to your face?"

"Let it go, Jimmy. Alright? Let me fix Marauder for you."

Next, I did something entirely out of my nature. I walked up to him and rested a hand on his shoulder. The touch sent a jolt through my body like I'd stuck a fork in a wall socket. I didn't let go, but I'm pretty sure my eyes went wide. I say that because Carlisle's eyes had gone wide too like he'd felt the lightning.

"Tell me what happened," I said.

Carlisle's eyes went back to their normal size. He smiled warmly. "Jimmy Allen, when you get something in your head, it sticks in there like a nettle, doesn't it? Sometimes it's best if you let it go. I'm fine. I promise."

I let go of his shoulder and took a few steps away, surveying the damage to my mighty vehicle.

"Can I at least help you with the tires?"

He handed me a tool and we got to it, Carlisle explaining every step along the way. I helped him cut bits of old rubber, and he showed me how to use a metal rod that looked like the end of a sewing needle to thread the black patch.

"And that's how it's done," he said when he'd finished the second tire.

"Can I try one on my own?"

"Big man," he said with a chuckle. He handed me the first tool, and I got to it. He didn't jump in unless I asked.

I was in the middle of trying to thread the patch when he asked, "Jimmy, what do you see when you look at me?"

"What do you mean?" I asked back, too focused on the

tire work to understand that a significant question lay at my feet.

"When you look at me, do you see a bad man? Someone who might hurt you?"

It took a few seconds for the shivers to hit my spine. My palms started to sweat. "Hurt me?"

Carlisle raised his hands to show that he'd meant nothing of the sort. "You know I wouldn't do that. It's just . . . ah, ignore me. I guess I'm feeling sorry for myself. Happens sometimes."

My nerve endings resettled. For the first time, I really looked at the man. The wide shoulders. The shaved face. The hands that could palm a basketball with enough grace left over to coax a tomato plant into growing straight.

"I see a prisoner," I said. Again, without thinking.

Carlisle nodded. "Me too. That's what I see every single day."

He paused, and I let him find the words. I was too dumb-struck to speak anyway.

"You spend enough time behind walls," he said, "and you start to believe the lie that you're less of a man. But I'm still a man. A good man." He squinted his eyes and nodded to no one when he said it. "I've worked hard to atone for my sins. I take care of people. I do my job. I never cause trouble."

He was staring at the ground, and I could about hear the wheels turning in his head.

"Carlisle, what's wrong?"

"I'm scared, Jimmy, that's all." He shook his head as if denying it.

"Scared of what?"

He shaped the air with his massive hands. "Hard to explain. You see, I thought the old me was long gone. Now I realize . . . let's say I'm scared he might come back again."

Think of something smart to say, Jimmy.

"Mom says we should live in the moment, you know, enjoy what we have."

Jimmy Allen, TED talker.

Carlisle chuckled. "Your mom's a smart lady, you know that? You'd be smart to listen to what she says."

"That's what she tells me."

We both laughed at that.

"You know, I never thought prison would make me a better man. Nope. I thought I'd be locked up here for good. I deserved it."

"What did you do?" Damn, blurts struck again.

If there was one thing Dad always drilled into our heads, it was we never were to ask an inmate what he'd done to be sent to prison. It wasn't our business. He said, "It was between the man, his Maker, and the law."

I don't think Carlisle knew Dad's rule. "It was drugs, mostly. Heroin. Smack, we call it. Though I did some more stuff that led me to get caught in the first place. Once they get you on a drug charge, they've got you for everything else." Now he looked at me and seemed to regard me as a fellow adult. "I was a dumb kid. I thought I could do anything without any of the consequences. Do you understand that, Jimmy?"

"I understand."

I wanted to tell him about seeing Dad's gun in the nightstand, and how there were days I felt like I wanted to grab it and take on the whole world—the Yancys, the Brady Bruces, the redcoats, all of them. I wanted to say that I wouldn't care what happened to me if I did. I didn't tell him that. But I had to let him know that I did understand.

"I put Larry in the fort on purpose," I said.

The regret of that damnable action still haunted me. I hadn't said a cross word to my little brother since.

"I know," Carlisle answered.

"How?"

"I just did."

"And you don't hate me?"

That stare again, like he could look into the very center of my swirling soul. "Now why the hell would you say that, Jimmy?"

"Because I could've gotten Larry killed."

"Yeah. You could have."

"Still, you don't hate me."

"It was a mistake. That's all I can see. It's not my place to judge. That's the work of the man upstairs."

"God?"

"Who'd you think I was talking about? Johnny Carson? Anyway, I know you didn't mean for your brother to get hurt."

"I didn't. I really didn't."

The tears came. Every ounce of remorse bubbled up and my sniffs turned to muffled sobs. I pulled up my shirt to wipe them.

Carlisle leaned in. "Jimmy, a man makes mistakes. It's what we do to atone for those mistakes that tells the world who we are. I see how you take care of Larry now. That boy loves you. You love him. Nothing better than that. You hold onto that. You know, I wish I'd loved my brother more."

It was the first I'd heard mention of any of Carlisle's family.

"What's his name?" I said, sob-sucking the words.

"My brother? His name was Cameron. We called him Cam."

"Carlisle and Cam," I mused aloud.

Carlisle chuckled. "You make us sound like a vaudeville act. Our mama thought it was cute."

The tape rewound in my head. *Was*.

"Is he still alive?"

Carlisle shook his head. "He died a year after I got in here."

"I'm sorry."

"Me too. Cam was a good kid. Always trying to be like me. That's what got him killed." That sentence hung in the air for some time before he spoke again. "I'm sorry. I shouldn't have told you that."

"You're goddamn right you shouldn't have told him anything, inmate."

Carlisle popped to his feet at the sound of Bruce's voice. Everything in me told me to run someplace far away.

Almost everything. I wasn't going to let my friend stay alone.

"Go home, kid," said Bruce. "This inmate and I have some business to discuss." He stepped forward and poked Carlisle in the chest with his stick. "Don't we, inmate?"

I wanted Carlisle to take the stick out of Bruce's hand and beat him with it. What he did instead, was say, "Run on home, Jimmy."

"But—"

Carlisle looked down at me, his eyes somehow bright and without a lick of concern. "Go. I'll be okay."

So, I ran. I ran so fast that if someone had stepped out in front of me, I'm pretty sure I'd have run through him.

All I remember hearing as I rounded the corner for our front door was a sound like a slap, and Bruce's voice saying, "If I catch you talking to that boy again, I'm going to kill you."

CHAPTER THIRTY-FOUR

Carlisle wasn't in the greenhouse the next day. He wasn't there on Monday morning before I went to school. I waited until the last possible second. He still didn't come.

Mom walked me to the bus that morning. She was jabbering on about something, I'm not sure what, and I didn't care. I was on the lookout for my friend. There were the roving patrols, the neighbors, the guards leaving the night shift. But no Carlisle.

Someone had to know. Perhaps Mom could wheedle her way in with Dad to find out. I stepped up onto the bus and turned to ask her if she could.

When I turned to ask the question, my eyes flicked to the house. Wouldn't you know it? Brady Bruce was holding Larry on his shoulders as Larry excitedly waved to me.

I froze, mouth hanging open.

"James. Honey, what is it?"

I should've pointed. I should've shouted. But I was a coward.

"All aboard, young man," said the bus driver.

I took one last look at Bruce. He winked comically at me,

an exaggerated gesture with a turned head and crooked mouth.

The bus doors closed, and I made my way to my assigned seat. Then I watched through the window as Larry giggled, riding on the monster's shoulders.

CHAPTER THIRTY-FIVE

That morning, the teacher called on me twice, and twice I begged off saying I didn't feel well.

"Do you need to go to the nurse?" she said.

"I think so," I said.

"Kenji, you go with him."

"Yes, Ma'am," Kenji said, quick on his feet.

The march to the nurse's office was slow and painful. The ache from my stomach had spread to my arms and legs. I wanted to fall to the ground and cry.

"Are you okay?" Kenji asked at some point along the way.

I wanted to tell him everything. He'd been my friend. My good friend. But what could he do? He hadn't even stood up to Yancy and his perverted pantsers.

"I'll be okay," I lied.

Kenji grabbed my arm and stopped us in the middle of the hall. "You're not sick. I know sick."

"What are you talking about? I am sick."

I met his eyes, and that's when he got me. There was a ferocity there. Not like he was mad at me for lying. More like he was going to get the truth no matter what I said. Something in me caved. I told him everything.

We made it to the nurse. She checked me up and down as thoroughly as a school nurse was allowed. When the nurse finished her examination, she said, "No fever. No symptoms. Why don't you lie down for a few minutes? Mr. Lawrence, why don't you head back to class."

"I'm supposed to stay with Jimmy."

She looked at us dubiously. "Keep quiet."

"We will," Kenji said.

The nurse left, and I lay back on the cot and closed my eyes. I wanted the world to disappear.

"Jimmy?" I heard.

"Yeah?" I said weakly.

"I have a plan."

I opened my eyes. "For what?"

"For Brady Bruce."

I propped myself up on my elbows. "What do you mean?"

"I mean, I think we can get him in trouble with your dad."

He had my attention. "How?"

He told me. I listened. When he was done, he stuck out his hand.

"Friends?"

I took his hand. It was firmer than I remembered. "Friends."

And then we settled in to plot the demise of Brady Bruce.

CHAPTER THIRTY-SIX

I t was a whole four days before we could arrange Kenji's visit. That gave us time to figure out some particulars. I did my part. I put on my old spy hat and took surreptitious notes as guards changed posts and patrols went by. I logged every sighting of Bruce.

Each morning I'd report in with Kenji, who'd go over my notes like a line editor combing a manuscript. He held a ball-point pen and clicked it every time he made a checkmark or underline, saying, "I think we can use this," or, "Yes. Just as I thought."

He didn't elaborate, and I didn't ask. I'd relegated myself to second in command. Kenji's mind was better suited for strategy. I was best suited for doing the dirty work. The man on the ground, slinking through the mud towards the target.

FRIDAY.

It took some heavy convincing on Kenji's part for his parents to agree to let us have a sleepover at my place. Kenji boarded the bus with me after school so off we went—going over our battle plans one last time.

I was giddy with nervous energy as we stepped off the bus. Kenji took it all in. The tree-lined drive. The log home at the end. The prison that was impossible to miss.

"Cool," he said as the bus pulled away. He paused for a moment, then looked at me and said, "Come on. We've got work to do."

We checked in with Mom first. "It's a pleasure to meet you, Kenji."

Kenji reached out his hand like a visiting dignitary. "Thank you for having me, Mrs. Allen."

That elicited a grin from Mom. "And so polite. Please make yourself at home."

To my surprise, she'd loaded the pantry with goodies we never had except during moves: my favorite cereals, snacks and desserts.

"I'm keeping strict inventory," she said, a playful wink in her voice.

We dropped our bags in my room and said a quick hello to Larry, who was in his own little world with robots and aliens. Afterward, we headed out the door. I gave Kenji the grand tour and showed him my four-wheeler that still had two flat tires. Soon after, I took him to the creek.

As much as I wanted to, I couldn't completely forget about Brady Bruce. He was always in the back of my mind, lingering there like a phantom. But our time in the water cleansed me of some of the bitterness. I wasn't alone. Kenji was back.

I showed him where the best spots were for catching

crawdads. He wasn't afraid of picking them up, even after he got pinched.

"In Japan, my grandfather would take me to the fish market. You should see how much fish they bring in every day."

"I'll bet it stinks."

"Not like you think. The fish is fresh like this little guy." He held the crawdad up by the torso, and it squirmed to bare its pincers. Kenji set it down in the water, and it swam away.

"You know you can hypnotize crabs by moving two fingers in front of them like this?" He demonstrated, pointing two fingers straight out and moving them in a slow, walking motion. "They go into a sort of trance and then you can wrap their claws in tape."

I thought "crab hypnotist" would one day make for an excellent occupation. I filed it away in the back of my mind for when I had to write my career day report.

"What's Japan like?" I asked, taking a seat on the edge of the creek bank, my feet kneading into the sandy bottom.

"My family lived outside Yokosuka. That's where the big American naval base is. There's a lot of people. Not like Tokyo, but still a lot. There's cool stuff there."

"When's the next time you're going back?"

His face made a strange, twisted expression. "We can't go to Japan again."

"Why not?"

He looked like he was going to answer the question. Instead, he said, "I'll bet I can catch more minnows than you."

And like that, the question was forgotten, and the race was on.

I ended up winning. Five minnows to Kenji's three. To be fair, I knew where to find them. He was a good sport, and I only did a little bragging. Ten is the bragging age. At ten, you come into your own. It's as if you have one chance and one chance only to prove you're a man.

We had our socks and shoes in our hands as we made our way home, our stomachs growling and our spirits high. The sun was coming down by then.

"Why do you think Bruce doesn't like you?" Kenji said.

"I don't know," I said, my soaring spirit losing several thousand feet in altitude. This comment had been the first mention of my nemesis in hours.

"What about the other guards? Is he friends with them?"

"I don't know," I said. "I mean, I've seen Bruce talking to the others, telling them stories. They seem like they like him, but I think they're . . . what's the word when you pretend you like someone?"

"Humoring them?"

"Yeah, that's it."

Kenji nodded thoughtfully. He may have been harboring the exact same wish for Bruce as I was—that the monster was a loner in life. It didn't seem fitting in the grand scheme of nature, that is, to have a guy like Bruce be well-liked in the least.

"It's not too late to back out, Jimmy," Kenji said suddenly.

"I know," I said, uneasy about the lack of confidence in his voice. This wasn't the Dungeon Master talking. This was the kid hanging from the bars with his pants around his ankles, his face redder than a British uniform.

The truth was, from the moment Kenji had proposed his *Get Back At Bruce Plan*, I was all in. More than all in. I had a vision of our coming victory.

Isn't there a saying about small men with big plans? Something about crashing to the ground with the pieces scattered around you? No?

There should be.

CHAPTER THIRTY-SEVEN

We had a rare family breakfast the next morning. Even Dad was there. Usually, he was gone by sun-up, and I'd sit with a bowl of cereal in front of the television. This Saturday morning, Mom was up and ready with pancakes, eggs, bacon, and a pitcher of fresh orange juice.

What was this sunrise elixir of life? She never bought orange juice that wasn't tipped out of a can with the sound of a cow pie hitting the pavement.

Dad had his arm around Mom's waist. He let go and turned to us when we came into the room.

"Ah. This must be Mr. Lawrence."

Kenji marched right over and stuck out his hand. "It's a pleasure to meet you, Mr. Allen."

I saw Dad's eyebrows go up. He took Kenji's proffered hand. "Pleasure to meet you too, Mr. Lawrence."

"You can call me Kenji, sir."

Now, Dad looked at me. "See that, James? Why can't you have manners like Kenji here?"

I let the comment go.

"Why don't you boys have a seat," said Mom, smoothing

the situation with maple syrup. "Kenji, would you like choco-late chips in your pancakes?"

"Yes, please, ma'am!"

"Jimmy?"

"Do we have any strawberries?"

She narrowed her eyes. "Now isn't that funny? I just happened to pick some up."

"I'll have strawberries, please."

Kenji leaned over to me and whispered, "Is this how it is every Saturday?"

"Not unless someone died."

Dad reached for the pack of cigarettes on the counter and shook out a single stick.

"Oh, please don't light up now, Dean," Mom said. "We have company."

"It's okay, Mrs. Allen. Lots of people smoke in Japan."

"Hear that, Esther? The Japanese are civilized people." He grabbed the cig with his teeth and lit it with a flick of his ever-present lighter. "Unlike the coddled idiots in this coun-try, a bunch of pansies afraid of their own shadows." He took a long drag. "My grandfather would be rolling over in his grave if he knew what was happening."

"Let it go, Dean. Who wants orange juice?"

"We're just having a conversation," he said through an exhaled cloud.

"No, *you're* just having a conversation."

I leaned in to Kenji. "This is more like a typical Saturday."

WE LEFT the house immediately after breakfast, our back-packs stuffed with supplies.

I led the way. Past the greenhouse. Past the sad four-wheeler. Past the other homes and our creek from the day before. We'd almost made it to our designated spot when I heard a call from behind.

"*James!*"

Dad came into view, Larry in tow. "You forgot your brother," he said when he'd reached us. Larry was wearing a small rucksack. He'd probably seen us and made a stink to tag along with a backpack, too. Only God knows what he had in it. Whatever it was, it, like the kid wearing it, wasn't part of the plan.

"Dad, Kenji and I . . ." I froze. Facing the warden wasn't easy.

"You and Kenji what?"

"Nothing, sir."

"Now you know I don't ask you this often, but I'd like for you to take your brother with you. Your mother and I have some things to discuss."

"We'll take good care of him, Mr. Allen," Kenji said.

"Good man, Kenji," said Dad.

Yeah, good man, Kenji.

Dad let go of my brother's hand. "Off you go then, Larry."

Larry immediately went for Kenji. "What are we playing?"

Like it was all in the script, Kenji said, "We're playing a game called *ambush*."

CHAPTER THIRTY-EIGHT

D-DAY.

I knew from my reconnaissance that there was one of only a few places we could hope to get Brady Bruce alone, a spot on a small rise near the farthest edge of the reservation boundary where patrol guards liked to park for a quick smoke. It had a terrific view of the countryside beyond the prison property. I'd been there myself a couple of times to watch the sunrise.

Kenji kept Larry busy finishing the hideout we'd started the day before. We had time. Not a lot. Breakfast had been a drawn-out event, but Kenji had added plenty of time for our prep in the initial planning stages. I was rehearsing my part in the drama. Timing and proper location were everything. We'd get one shot. Just one. I did not want to mess this one up. It was my one chance to get rid of my arch-nemesis and get Carlisle back to his rightful place on our staff.

The truck came rumbling up the two-run path as the lunch whistle faded into the distance. I held my breath as it came closer. I'd been calm up to that point, but now my legs felt like Jell-O, and my insides squirmed like a thousand centipedes.

"Ready?" Kenji asked. He had the video camera on his shoulder. Larry kept looking back and forth between us. Kenji had sworn my brother to silence. I was amazed that Larry actually listened. He hadn't let out a peep in close to ten minutes. I knew because I'd been counting down every second.

My heart thudded in my ears, and my hands began to cramp.

"Here," Kenji said, handing me my weapon.

Something about the solidity of the object gave me strength.

The truck was about fifty yards away now.

"It's time," Kenji said, his eye fixed behind the eyepiece of the camera.

I took a deep breath, took one last look at my brother, then marched out to meet Brady Bruce head-on.

CHAPTER THIRTY-NINE

The plan was to appear in the middle of the road and make my stand—a steadfast warrior facing down the enemy in a grand show of courage and self-assurance.

I stepped into the road and tripped over a clump of dried mud. Tumbling once, then springing up in time to see the truck stop. Too soon. Too far away.

I steadied myself. I saw the red hair in the driver's seat, the cigarette dangling out of the corner of the mouth.

I clutched the object in my hand and judged the distance. Too far.

Bruce stuck his head out the window, the cigarette bobbing as he said, "What are you doing, kid?"

I had nothing to offer in response. Now, all the words I'd rehearsed stuck in my fluttering stomach like dragonflies in tar. So instead of talking, I did the only thing that came to mind. I gave Brady Bruce the middle finger from my non-weaponed hand.

The truck's engine revved, and the old beast was grinding closer. My knees were knocking now. If this didn't go as

planned—that is, if Bruce didn't do what Kenji said he'd do—
I was dead meat walking.

When I gauged that the truck was within range, I let my
weapon fly. It was a perfect throw. Just perfect. The rock hit
the smack dab center of the windshield.

Vengeance was mine!

Only there was none.

No crack. No shattering of glass. No glory.

The truck stopped, and Bruce put it in park and was out
the door. This was it. It would all be on film. We'd gotten
Bruce to fly into a blood-spattering frenzy of anger.

Only not really.

We wanted hellfire rage. Bruce gave us mild annoyance.

"Now why'd you go and do that, kid?"

"Fuck you, Bruce!" I put as much venom as I could into
the words.

Bruce took an extra-long drag and flicked the cooked
cigarette off to the side of the road. A streak of red embers
followed its arc. I steeled myself for the coming confronta-
tion. I had to be brave.

"That's some mouth you've got there," Bruce said. What
the hell was wrong with this guy?

Desperation time.

"Did you hear me?" I said, my voice squeaking.

"I heard you. Why don't you run on home before I call
your parents? Do they even know you're out here?"

That got my blood up. It was one thing to treat me like
the ten-year-old I was; it was another to tell me where I
should or should not be. I was Warden Allen's son. My pride
bubbled forth.

"I know what you did, you sonofabitch!" I yelled. "And
we're gonna get you fired!"

The words came out so fast I hadn't had time to fix them.
I knew my mistake immediately.

"We?"

"I mean me," I corrected.

Bruce fished the pack out of his pocket. Another cigarette appeared in his hand. He lit it slowly, and I watched every micro movement. The flick. The flame. The catch. The inhale. The puff.

"Maybe I'll take a look around, make sure there isn't anything to get you in trouble."

Just then, Larry burst from our hiding spot. I heard Kenji whisper a harsh warning, but my brother didn't listen. Larry made a beeline to me. He looked at Bruce without an ounce of fear. Larry had his hands on his hips like I'd seen Dad do a thousand times. He looked like Dad. He *was* Dad.

Larry pointed his finger at the big man and said, "You leave my brother alone, Mr. Bruce. I'm gonna tell my mom on you."

Now that set the fire head off. The roaring laugh burst from Bruce's lungs and went on for a good minute, maybe longer. He bent over, hands on his knees, and struggled for breath.

"You've got balls, little man," he said. "You James, you should take lessons from your kid brother. Good God, I think my chest is gonna burst!"

He was still laughing like a mule when he drove off, giving us a two-fingered salute as he did.

Just like that, Operation Tank Brady Bruce faded like spit on a blacktop.

CHAPTER FORTY

"Maybe I can splice something together," said Kenji. He'd been trying to mollify me all afternoon. I could not be quelled for all the Snickers in Candyland.

"Seriously. My dad has a friend who edits VHS tapes at his house."

"Rat bastard," I said.

"Language, James," Mom said from the kitchen. She was making another feast in honor of our guest.

"Rat bastard," I said again, softly.

Kenji was fiddling with the video camera, and I was staring at the ceiling when the doorbell rang. I jumped to my feet.

"It's Brady Bruce," I said, my body tingling with anticipation.

"Maybe it's not." Kenji lay the camera down and got to his feet. I saw him flinch at the act, but I didn't ask why.

I heard Mom's voice and the murmuring of a man.

"Come on," I said.

We snuck our way to the front room.

"I'll tell him you came by," Mom said and closed the front door.

"Who was it?" I asked, my voice thin with anticipation.

"It was Carlisle," she said, her voice uneasy.

"Why'd you say it like that?"

"Well, because . . . because Carlisle didn't look well."

"What did he want?" I said, testing the boundaries of spy hood.

"He wanted to talk to your father."

"About what?"

Mom threw me one of those looks. "That's your father's business."

"But I just ask—"

"Question time is over, James. You and Kenji go wash up. Dinner's almost ready."

We retreated to my room. I closed the door, so Mom couldn't hear.

"You have to cover for me," I said, slipping on my shoes.

"Where are you going?" Kenji asked, alarmed.

"I have to talk to Carlisle."

He heard it in my voice. I would not be swayed.

"What should I tell your mom?"

"You're the smart one," I said. "You'll think of something."

The spy was back in full form, out the window and sprinting before my feet hit the deck.

I CHECKED THE GREENHOUSE FIRST. Empty.

I patted the flattened four-wheeler as I sped by. Poor Marauder. We shall have our bloody revenge soon.

I was about a hundred yards from the front gate when I saw him.

"Carlisle," I whispered.

He was slow to turn like the very act took a considerable effort. I'm pretty sure I gasped when he finally faced me.

Ever see what an orb spider does to a beetle? It was like that. Everything had drained from the man, and nothing was left but a flaking shell in its place. I hadn't realized until then how much of Carlisle's physical appearance was made up of sheer confidence alone. There wasn't even a ghost of it left.

"Jimmy?"

"Carlisle?" I said again, my voice wavering. "Are you okay?"

"I'm fine."

I went a few steps closer, fighting the urge to go and hug him. He looked like he'd break from it. Or maybe I would.

"You're hurt."

"No one hurt me."

"Yeah, *he* did."

"Let it be, Jimmy."

"Bruce."

Anger flashed in Carlisle's eyes and was gone just as quick. "I said, *let it be*."

He turned to go. I grabbed his hand, cold and lifeless.

"Carlisle," I said again, tears beginning to well in my eyes. Dammit, Jimmy, you're a man, not a little girl.

I felt him shudder. "You stay clear of me, Jimmy."

"Where are you going?"

He wouldn't look at me now, but he didn't let go of my hand. "I came to tell your dad that I'm volunteering for laundry duty. They need help getting things in line. And besides, it's my time."

He started to let go of my hand. I wouldn't let him. "You can't give up. You can't. You said we were friends."

Now he turned.

"We *are* friends, Jimmy. It's just... aw hell, Jimmy."

"You're giving up. You're letting Bruce win."

He exhaled. I could see he was looking for the right words to dump on a kid. "It's complicated, Jimmy. You wait 'til you're a little older, then you'll understand."

That bugged me. My tears stilled, I said, "I'm old enough, dammit."

"I can't," he said and pried my hand from his.

"Carlisle."

"Take care of yourself, Jimmy."

And that was that. Carlisle was gone, and I was alone. I couldn't hear the birds or the rustling squirrels. I cared for nothing. Not the fort, not exploring the grounds, not the crawdads in the creek or the faded, distant summer; not Marauder, or Warden Allen, or the Dungeon Master, or goddammed George Washington.

The only thing that mattered at that moment was that Brady Bruce had taken my friend.

CHAPTER FORTY-ONE

Days went by, misery being my only company.

Kenji tried. He asked to spend time at my house. He invited me to his. I brushed each and every invitation away.

When I wasn't at school practicing educational self-destruction, I was at home moping, waiting for some glimpse of Carlisle. I got nothing. Nothing on patrols. No whispers from the guards passing by. One day, the mystery got to be too much. I saw Harley ambling up toward the greenhouse and ran after him.

"Harley!" I called.

He stopped and did a half-turn, saw it was me, then continued walking.

"Hey, Harley!" I repeated.

"Why are you always underfoot?"

"Where's Carlisle?"

He turned away. "I ain't the warden, kid."

"Come on, Harley," I said as I caught up to him and grabbed hold of his sleeve. "Is he okay?"

He looked at me like he didn't know whether he could

trust me. I didn't like that look one bit. Then he shook his head and said, "Best not to talk about it." He brushed off my arm, told me to get on home, and that was the end of the discussion.

I saw Brady Bruce soon after. I hadn't planned on a meeting. He was heading back from lunch and caught my eye. I stared mouth agog like some bumpkin from the low country.

"Well," he said with a jovial smile. "If it ain't Killer Allen, the terror of Virginia. Afternoon, Killer." He tipped his hat like a country sheriff doing rounds and went on his way.

SLOWLY, very slowly, a plan formed in my mind. At first, it was the idle daydreaming of a boy in pain. But thoughts had a way of solidifying in my life. This one began as small as a pebble, morphed into a quarter-sized dream, then kept on swelling. It was orange, a basketball, then a house. Soon, the idea became the only thing that could keep my interest.

You may not know what it's like to become taken hold of by a single obsession. But I do, because of the way that plan usurped all my thoughts at the time. Now, these many years later, I can understand addicts and alcoholics, and I can see underneath the crazed ramblings of religious zealots. And prisoners. They were held in place by iron and concrete. I was held in place by a mind that could focus on nothing else besides the undoing of my greatest enemy.

I decided to apply myself in my schoolwork, if only partially, and for no other reason than to keep my parents at bay and give me more time to work on my idea.

But late at night, when sleep came in fits and starts, my idea fed on the surreal morsels my dreams left for it, a breadcrumb trail leading me to the dark side of my soul.

CHAPTER FORTY-TWO

The roving patrol came to a stop next to my now fixed four-wheeler. I waved to the guard and plastered what I thought was a more than a passable smile on my face. The new me did not smile unless he had to: all part of the plan.

"Good morning, Jimmy," said the guard, a middle-aged man named Skip. He was pleasant if a bit dense. They didn't let him near any of the prison's hard cases. Patrols were okay enough for Skip.

"You're up early." He spat a glistening stream of tobacco to the grass.

"Wanted to get a ride in before the snow."

Skip looked up at the sky and shivered. "I don't know how you northerners live with the snow. Me here, well, I'm happy with hot, hot, hot."

He laughed, and I with him.

That was the thing about being the warden's son. Everyone got a turn at kissing your butt, and this was Skip's turn, and he knew it, so he nodded once and moved along.

I watched the truck go. Waited. Watched. Waited some more.

Coast clear.

I revved the four-wheeler to life. It purred under me for a moment, then roared, and I gunned the engine.

Skip's truck stopped at Pat Garvey's house to pick up laundry. Funny story there.

I'd overheard Mom on the phone one day.

"Well, she's got no business running a home. Yes, it's true . . . really, did you . . . no!"

This tone of hers, the kind a mother uses when there's something juicy on the other end of the phone line, was like dangling a candy bar in front of me. I backed up to the wall and listened to the rest of the conversation.

"Yes, well, we were there about a week ago. We'd sat down to have a glass of sweet tea? Alma pulls out this awful-looking sponge. I mean . . ."

Alma. This was Alma Garvey, no doubt.

"And she wipes out the glass with this nasty rag and hands it to me as if I'd think it was perfectly fine to drink out of it. Ugh! And the laundry . . . yes, you did . . . how? I don't know how Pat can stand it. He had a stain on his pants that could only be mustard, and I swear it was a week old."

I don't know why I thought it necessary to tell Harley about it. It was one of those things I blabbed out while hanging around him while he worked. I thought he was half-listening.

My only guess is that Harley told someone else about it, maybe a guard, who knows?

Then, well, you know how these things get around.

Pretty soon, because of your humble servant's prying ears and big mouth, The Garveys began sending their laundry out to be cleaned by the inmates, who had plenty of time to spend on mustard stains.

Once the Garveys hopped on the laundry train, two other

families hopped on too. Skip was there to pick the laundry up. This was the last of three stops.

Dad always said that a routine was bad. Routine makes you lax. Routine exposes your weaknesses. I used that to my advantage, of course. A good spy always exposes weaknesses. General Washington would have been proud. The audacity of my plan. Yes.

I watched Skip take the overstuffed laundry bags from Mrs. Garvey. She was pregnant again and didn't look so hot. I had no idea what women went through in pregnancy and didn't care. All I knew was that her condition helped my plan along.

"Have a nice day," she said with mock cheer, one hand on her stomach and her face the color of an old frog. Then her eyes went wide. She pressed a hand to her mouth and rushed back inside.

Skip shook his head in commiseration, then stacked the laundry bags on top of the others. He closed the tailgate and whistled his way back to the driver's seat. As usual, he didn't get in the truck until he pulled another pinch of chaw from his Levi Garrett pouch and stuck it in his cheek. Like he always did. Routine. Your worst enemy. My best friend.

I made my move, timing my climb into the truck bed perfectly. I was probably too light to make the truck bed buck, but it made sense to time my climbing to match Skip getting into the cab. He never looked in the rearview mirror, nor turned around. He slid the keys into the ignition, turned the engine over and pressed the gas twice. Just like every time before.

Then we were off. Me covered in cloth laundry bags, smelling the stink of three families, and Skip humming along with the radio.

The truck stopped at the gate, and I heard Skip making small talk with the gate guard.

"What's that song, Skip?"

"A new one. Something about a prayer. The group's called Banjo Jehovah."

"Who?"

"Banjo Jehovah?"

"Ban—Jehovah? You mean *Bon Jovi*, you idiot?"

"Who?"

"Bon Jovi. That's the name of the band."

"Huh. Well, that makes no sense."

"Livin' On A Prayer" crooned from the radio as I held my breath. I heard the crunch of footsteps as the gate guard did a whirl around the truck.

"You're good to go, Skip." The guard patted the side of the truck, a move that made my skin prickle all over. "You better turn that radio off before you go inside."

"I know, I know. Wouldn't want the warden to catch me."

The radio clicked off, and on we rumbled. I heard the squeak of the gates closing behind us. I parted two laundry bags to the slightest slit to make myself a peephole and saw the guard refocused on the outside.

And just like that, I'd snuck into the prison. Operation Find Carlisle was a go.

CHAPTER FORTY-THREE

The truck came to a stop outside the laundry facility. The tumble of washers and dryers greeted us as the garage doors slid open. The radio clicked off.

"Hey, Skip," someone said.

"Have you seen the warden around?" Skip asked.

"Nope."

"All's well then?"

"Just a squirrel lookin' for a nut."

"I hear you. Catch you on the flipside."

Grownups and their codes.

The radio clicked on again and in we went, slipping deeper inside the laundry sanctum.

I'd only been in one laundry facility before. It was hot and smelled like that nauseating combination of detergent and filth with the sharp smell of bleach everywhere. It was loud, the thrumming of machines and a steady, dull *boom, boom, boom;* like being trapped inside a bass drum. But the noise and the heat made it a perfect place for dirty deeds.

The truck came to another stop. Here's where I was betting that Skip would help me again. It worked.

First, he opened the tailgate. But instead of immediately unloading the laundry, or having one of the inmates do it for him, Skip went to find someone that would gab with him. Perfect. I'd chosen Skip because I knew he had a head full of cream cheese and liked to talk. So far, so predictable.

I peeked out further, making my peephole bigger and bigger as I rearranged my hiding spot. No one in the immediate vicinity. One small problem: I hadn't accounted for my thudding heart.

Come on you wimp, I thought. *Do it for Carlisle*.

If I got caught, I'd get throttled for sure. Possibly punished in a way that would hurt beyond the initial physical phase of discipline—I'd be grounded or have Marauder taken away for good. Not only that, there had to be some crime listed in the formidable annals of the Federal Bureau of Prisons.

Infraction, 3829: Impersonating Laundry.

My overactive imagination settled on the pleasant thought that the meanest inmate in the entire penal world would find me and do terrible things. At that age, I had no idea what that meant; however, I only had to conjure up the worst monsters from Kenji's D&D adventures to give me a clue. Whatever they did to me, it would involve fire and something sharp, and wielded with the greatest expertise.

I slid out of the truck bed backward on my belly. No one around and smack dab in the middle of a prison.

And that's when your humble servant committed his next mistake. How the hell was I going to get out?

I found a spot behind an especially loud dryer. The rumble and jangle made my teeth rattle.

Then, there was only one thing to do: stand here and think. And wait.

CHAPTER FORTY-FOUR

Third mistake: no watch.

I couldn't tell if time was running fast or slow. Meanwhile, my clothes were soaking with sweat. It was hot. Not like ninety-degree baking in the Virginia sun hot. No. This was getting locked in a sauna after someone dumped a bucket of water on hot coals hot. My throat felt like I'd swallowed a wool blanket. The possibility of getting caught was the only thing keeping me from focusing too hard on my thirst.

Skip had already left with the truck and had taken his sweet time in the process. I knew the inmates liked him. Everyone wants someone to gab with—to connect and sometimes laugh. He was a bit too casual with them. Dad probably wouldn't have approved. Nevertheless, he finally did his job and left me as the only civilian in the bowels of the beast.

Inmates came and went. Sometimes it was one or two. At other times, it was a gaggle. The pace felt languid like being surrounded by bees caught in sap in late August.

Then I saw him.

Carlisle pushed a wheeled canvas laundry basket overflowing with prison uniforms. I wanted to jump from my hiding spot and run to him. I needed to tell him that I was there to save him. That was the plan, wasn't it? But how in the world was I supposed to do that?

Again, I hadn't exactly planned that far. To be totally honest, I hadn't thought I'd get much past the front gate.

But I was there now, and I had to make the best of it.

Carlisle passed from view. There was enough room to wiggle behind the dryer and on to the next. Then another. And another.

There he was. An armload of clothing went into the washer, one at a time. Carlisle was wearing a stained tank top, drenched. Every inch of his exposed skin was glistening with sweat.

I was close now—maybe eight or nine feet. Yet, I'd still have to shout if I wanted my friend to hear me, and that might bring other inmates. I couldn't risk that.

I moved a step closer, as far as I dared to go before exposing myself. My foot crunched on something. I lifted my foot and found the remnants of someone's lunch. A few crackers littered the floor.

I picked up two whole bits and looked back and forth. Coast was clear.

The first cracker I threw like a baseball. It fell three feet short of my target.

The next I readied to throw like a frisbee. A blubbering fat inmate appeared as I wound up. His chest was bare and covered in curly black hair like he was wearing the skin of a bear with a perm.

"Whatdya say, Carlisle?" the man shouted. He had a cigarette stuck behind one ear, nearly covered by hair that matched his chest. "You running a meeting tonight?"

"Not tonight. Too much to do."

The inmate's arm rested on a bin, and his fat sloshed leeward.

"The boys miss you; you know. It's not the same without you."

"Too busy."

The man stared at Carlisle but received no further explanation.

"Let me know if you need anything, buddy." He patted Carlisle's back like they were friends. There was real affection there.

The inmate left, and Carlisle moved on to the next washing machine. I had one cracker left. After that, the only thing I could do was shout for his attention, or try to sneak from my hiding spot. Neither option was tempting. More than one prisoner had already appeared out of nowhere. There were too many angles of approach. Too many places I couldn't see.

I took aim and threw. The cracker went left, maybe pushed by a swirl of unseen air. I was about to groan when the projectile turned right in a natural curve and hit Carlisle in the middle of the back.

He didn't move.

Then, ever so slowly, Carlisle turned. He saw the cracker on the ground. His eyes were slits, and he looked left, then right.

I took a chance and waved. The movement caught his attention.

He squinted, and I showed my face from the shadows. His eyes went wide, but he didn't immediately come over. Instead, he finished his current load, started the machine, then picked up another armful of soiled clothing.

I really thought he was going to ignore me. He didn't.

He came my way. My body flooded with relief.

His body cast a shadow over mine.

"What the hell are you doing here, Jimmy?"

His eyes flicked back and forth, never really locking onto mine. I wanted our eyes to meet. I wanted to see that it was really him. I can't explain why. Maybe part of me thought his mind and body had been taken over by aliens. I don't know.

"I wanted to make sure you were okay."

"Do you know what kind of trouble you could get me in?"

"I know. I'm sorry." The line cut. Up until now, I'd only been thinking about the trouble *I* could get in.

Now his eyes met mine. It wasn't the kind, understanding look I'd come to rely on. It was anger, pure and unfiltered, like a battered boxer leveling whatever spite he had left at his opponent.

I must've taken a step back because he reached out for me, held me in place.

"You shouldn't be here, Jimmy."

"I know," I said again. Now that I was here, I had no idea what to say. I'd prepped speech after speech. They were all stuck in whatever place a person's oratory goes to die.

A voice boomed above the tumult. Carlisle's face tightened, and my body went slack with dread.

It was Brady Bruce. And he was coming.

CHAPTER FORTY-FIVE

I cowered behind the dryer as Carlisle went back to his task. I tried to shrink smaller when Bruce appeared.

No way I could hear what the sadist was saying. He poked Carlisle in the chest, punctuating whatever he was saying time after time.

The stick went back in its holster, and Bruce cracked his neck back and forth. Then he left.

I was moving out of my hiding spot when Bruce appeared again, ghostlike. His strike was fast.

The first blow hammered Carlisle's lower back. That made him arch back. It had been so quick that I only had time to gasp.

The second swat with the nightstick whipped his front, doubling Carlisle over.

Spittle trickled onto the floor. Bruce held his hands in the air like a conquering warrior. Then he grasped the stick using both of his hands; the dark knight about to slay his opponent.

I did the only thing my mind and body would allow.

I screamed.

CHAPTER FORTY-SIX

If I was trying to make a scene, it worked. It felt like the gears of the prison jammed to full stop.

Bruce's face whipped my way, arms still raised in the air.

"Leave him alone!" I screamed; my voice much higher than the baritone for which I had been hoping. At least the fear was gone, swept away by anger and concern for my friend.

Carlisle reached one of his hands out, and Bruce batted it down with fury. I saw the wrist snap and Carlisle's face contorted in pain. He went down to one knee.

I was all raging fury now. As an adult, I know the feeling. Bloodlust. Back then, all I knew was that I wanted more of it —more rage, more fury. I ran at Bruce, not knowing or caring about what I would do next.

He turned to receive me, hands by his sides. There was a smile on his hateful face.

My ten-year-old mind did quick math. I couldn't reach Bruce's face, and his torso was hard as a rock. I'd probably break my hand. So, I went with what every boy knew to be the sweet spot. Dead aim. *Say goodbye to any prospect of having children, you bastard.*

I was a hair's breadth from my target when Bruce planted a hand on the top of my head and held me at arm's length. I turned into a trapped, flailing beast. I grabbed his wrist and bit into his hand. Warm, coppery blood flowed into my mouth.

"Ow! You little son of a bitch! Stop that!"

A slap came to the side of my head, and I spun to the ground with its stinging pain. My face tingled and then burned. My jaw locked momentarily. My eyes blurred. I could barely make out Bruce's form through the tears, but I pushed past it.

Then I stood, shakily. And I ran at Bruce again. And this time, I hit dead center. He bent at the middle when my double fist hit. Nothing left to do now but *squeeze*.

Brady Bruce squealed like a pig. It was like hearing an angel's song.

Then something crashed into the back of my head, and my world spiked black.

CHAPTER FORTY-SEVEN

I came to slowly.

I thought I heard voices through the fog. The pain was everywhere, radiating like a nuclear reactor from the back of my head. Even the tips of my toes hurt.

"Hey, he's coming around."

"Lie still now, Jimmy."

"Brave little shit," the first voice said again.

"Watch your mouth." *Was that Carlisle's voice?*

One eye came open, and I snapped it closed just as fast.

"I know it hurts, Jimmy, but you have to wake up."

My hand probed the back of my injured head for a gaping wound. In one of Kenji's D&D adventures, we were attacked by an orc wielding what I eventually learned was called a mace. I was sure someone had clobbered me with one. There was a lump there the size of an egg. But no blood. That was good.

Then the memory flooded back.

"Bruce," I said, my body spasming to a sitting position. Everything swirled. My ears rang with a high keen.

"It's okay," Carlisle said.

That's when I noticed the absence of the laundry racket.

"Where are we?"

"Somewhere safe."

"For now," the stranger's voice said.

I looked up to see the fat man from before towering over me. All my senses swirled back as the man's body odor assaulted me. I looked past him and saw others. Old. Young. Hunched and straight. All staring.

I backed up and bumped against a wall.

"It's okay," Carlisle said. "No one's gonna hurt you."

"Yeah, but Bruce might lick us all," one from the gallery said.

"Maybe we should kill him."

"Don't be stupid. You're in here for forging checks."

"Then I say we kick him in the balls a few more times. No sense letting that bastard breed."

There were murmurs of agreement.

Carlisle raised a hand stopping the back and forth.

"We need to get you home, Jimmy," he said.

"I don't know if I can walk."

And I meant it. My stomach churned, and I knew I was going to puke. Luckily, I aimed left. What was left of breakfast splattered to the floor.

"Now who's gonna clean that up?" one of the inmates whined.

"You're gonna clean it up," the fat man said to the whiner, his tone leaving zero room for refusal. "We've gotta get moving before Bruce wakes up."

"Did I knock him out?" I asked.

There was a collective chuckle.

"You did your best, kid. Really, you did," the fat man said, his belly jiggling Jell-O. "I had to take him out with a mop. Took a couple of hits, but he's out."

"You'll get in trouble," I said.

"Would you look at that," someone said. "The kid gives more of a shit about us than himself. Crazy little fucker."

"I said, watch your mouth."

"Oh, hey, sorry. I didn't realize we had the Duke of York sitting here."

Another urge to vomit coursed up my esophagus. I choked it back. My world swayed like a teeter-totter.

"We should get him checked out," the fat man said.

"No time," Carlisle said.

"Fine, but we need to get him out of here, now. Last call is in an hour."

"Yeah, what's the plan, Carlisle?" another man asked.

"I'm thinking."

"Well, think faster. I'm hungry."

The fat man spun and stomped toward the peanut gallery. I saw them scatter to the shadows.

"I'm sorry," I said, knowing I'd surely stepped in it this time.

"You don't need to be sorry, Jimmy. It's the nicest thing anyone has done for me."

"But I can't get out—"

"You let me worry about that. Well, me, Chef, and God."

"Who's Chef?"

"I'm Chef," the fat man said, back from chasing off the witnesses. He reached down a sweaty hand. "Pleased to meet a friend of Carlisle's." He let go and wiped his soaked forehead with the back of his arm. "You know I'm all for pleasantries Carlisle, but we're gonna need a plan, and fast."

That's when I saw the old Carlisle again. Confident. Sure. In the moment.

"We get him outta here. That's the plan."

CHAPTER FORTY-EIGHT

"You stay down," said Carlisle.

I didn't like the plan: not one bit. But I nodded to Carlisle anyway, even though I wanted to run. Probably not the best idea considering my pounding headache and wobbly legs.

"What about Bruce?" I asked.

"I'd seen what they did to him. Tied him up like a pig going to slaughter." Carlisle continued, "He won't say a word. Wouldn't help his growing reputation around here."

"I don't understand."

Carlisle grasped my forearm. "Let's say he has more to lose than we do. Let's say we don't think your dad would take kindly to one of his guards hitting his son. What do you think?"

"I don't know," I said. "Brady Bruce is a liar, and people believe him when he lies. And no one believes a kid. Or an—" I stopped myself.

A soft smile appeared on Carlisle's face. "You can say it. No one believes a prisoner. You're right. Life might get a little tough for the rest of us. But the next time I see you at the greenhouse, things are going to be fine."

"The greenhouse? How?"

Carlisle chuckled. A welcome sound considering the circumstances. "I'm asking your dad for my job back. Well, as a matter of fact, he's asked me to come back."

"Wait. When?"

"I'd say ten times since I left. Your father's a good man, Jimmy. The best warden I've had the pleasure of serving under."

There was built-in respect that the job commanded. But I'd never heard anyone voice respect because they *meant* it.

If Carlisle was coming home, everything would be okay, even if Bruce was still on the loose.

"Promise me you won't leave again," I said.

"How about we take it one day at a time?"

I couldn't argue with that. The warmth radiating from Carlisle gave me faith in the future. I still can't explain the calm that man imbued. It was the only thing that gave me the courage to ride in the back of the truck soon to be driven by Brady Bruce.

CHAPTER FORTY-NINE

Bruce appeared, surrounded by the same group of inmates from my awakening. To his credit, he looked ninety percent of his cocky self. You couldn't even tell he'd been knocked out and trussed like an animal.

"Now you remember the deal, Mr. Bruce," said Carlisle. "Jimmy gets home, and none of this gets back to the warden."

I expected a comeback, one with the bite of a jackal. None came. Bruce nodded his head and got into the driver's seat.

I didn't understand the politics that went along with the play. To me, the bad man was free and could do whatever he wanted. That scared me to shivers.

The truck rumbled to life, and off we went. I didn't dare budge an inch within my hiding spot. Carlisle waved to me. His smiling image was the only thing that got me home sane.

"Hey, Bruce," the new gate guard hailed. "A little early for your rounds, aren't you?"

"Gotta take the laundry back to Warden Allen's house."

The guard whistled.

"Must be nice to have same day service. Never heard of it myself."

No reply came from Bruce, just the squeal of the gate opening.

I swear the air felt lighter on the outside. I breathed in great gulps of it. Never mind the smell of cheap laundry detergent all around. I was free again.

The gate passed behind us. The guard went back to whatever it was he was reading. I readied myself for a quick exit. I wasn't going to give Bruce the chance to go back on his word, no matter what Carlisle said.

But we didn't turn right; we went left instead toward the town and a bunch of nothing.

I thought about jumping from the truck; however, we were going too fast. I'd either kill myself trying or get the world's worst case of road rash. Neither option felt viable.

On and on we went. I wanted to move. I wanted to see what Bruce was doing.

Finally, we slowed, and I got ready to bolt. Worst case, I could walk home from wherever we were.

The engine gunned again, and plumes of dust kicked up behind us. We were on a back road. Maybe a farm road. Trees appeared the next moment as if we'd gone under a tunnel. It was too early to be this dark.

I was beginning to move the brown paper wrapped packages of clothing when the pick-up swerved left so suddenly that my head slammed against the side of the truck. I reeled, too dazed to make my escape.

Bruce was looming over me before I could take a breath. He picked me up by the front of my shirt and hoisted me out of the truck bed.

"You think you're a smart little shit, don't you?" he hissed. "Answer me!"

I shook my head. "I'm not smart." The tears were coming.

"That's right. You're not smart. You're a stupid little fucker that sticks his head into business that isn't his. I should strangle you and leave you to rot."

"Then do it," I said, barely gasping out the words with his fist pushing against my windpipe.

"I will!"

"Do it," I said again.

Strange. I had no fear. Yes, I was crying. There was too much anger for my ten-year-old heart to contain, and it threatened to burst from my chest and shook my entire body. I had no other recourse but to cry because of it. However, I wasn't scared. I was pissed beyond words.

He stared at me for a long time. I felt the tremble of his body as his jaw moved without speaking as if gnawing on something invisible.

"You have no idea," he said. "All the planning. All the goddammed *planning*."

I didn't have the breath to ask him what the hell he was talking about. All I knew was that I was choking, and Bruce wasn't going to stop. I grabbed his wrists, and that's when he slammed me against the truck. Whatever oxygen I had left was purged from my lungs in a sharp wheeze.

I was suddenly scared.

CHAPTER FIFTY

I tried to lock glares with him, willing the same fierceness he had in his eyes. Nothing: just the fear that spread to every inch of me. Something warm trickled down my left leg.

Bruce looked down and grinned.

"You pissed yourself, you little shit."

He held me farther away, and the move gave me more room to breathe. My lungs ached for the O_2.

"Let me go," I wheezed, snot dripping from my nose.

Bruce leaned his face in real close, so our foreheads were touching. His ashtray breath overwhelmed my senses.

"If I ever catch you snooping around again . . ."

He didn't have to say more. I saw murder in his eyes.

"I promise," I said.

He let me go with a shove, and it was over.

Brady Bruce–1.

Pee-stained-blubber-baby–0.

CHAPTER FIFTY-ONE

He dropped me at the greenhouse without a word. I ran home out of breath, needing the smell and feel of something familiar.

"Is that you, James?" Mom asked from the kitchen when I came inside.

"Yes, Ma'am."

"Where were you today? Your brother was looking for you."

"I was just out."

Mom never pressed. She must have figured that as long I wasn't sticking my fingers into light sockets or licking wild toads, I was alright doing whatever it was that boys were supposed to do.

"Get cleaned up. Supper will be on the table in fifteen minutes."

"Yes, Ma'am."

Luckily, she didn't come to the living room. Luckily, she didn't see my soiled pants. Luckily, my dad worked late.

I made it to my room and hurried to strip down to my underwear. A shower sounded better than heaven.

Pissed-on pants in hand, I was about to close the bathroom door when Larry appeared.

"What were you doing with Mr. Bruce?" he said.

CHAPTER FIFTY-TWO

"What are you talking about?" I asked, closing the door so Larry couldn't see what was in my hands.

"You were in the back of the truck. Mr. Bruce was driving. Did he take you on a ride?"

There was no way around this. Larry would forget this very conversation right after we had it, or he would keep bringing it up for days.

What to say?

"If I tell you, promise not to tell Mom and Dad?"

His ran two fingers across his mouth like he was zipping it shut.

"Mr. Bruce showed me a new hiding spot. Best hiding spot you've ever seen. I wanted it to be a surprise, but—"

"Oh, I won't say anything, Jimmy. I promise."

I looked at him like Mom looked at me when she was sure I was telling a fib. "I don't believe you."

He made an X over his chest. "Cross my heart and hope to die."

"Okay. How about we go tomorrow, after school?"

"Yeah!"

"*Shhh.*"

"Sorry," he said quieter now. "I promise I won't tell, Jimmy."

"Good. Now go away. I want to take a shower."

One problem dealt with so, I closed the door and leaned against it. My head ached. My body had rebelled. My brain kicked like a stubborn mule braying at its master.

The shower did little to soothe my twisted nerves. It did clean me of my own filth.

I was careful to rinse my pants, socks, and underwear, so there would be no proof for my over-inquisitive mother. I could hang them outside my bedroom window, and they'd be almost dry by the time Dad came home.

Just like George Washington, I thought, hiding piss pants from his parents after a day facing down the enemy. I cursed the idea, got dressed, and headed toward supper in a disgraceful, defeated daze.

CHAPTER FIFTY-THREE

When I got to school the next day, all I wanted to do was tell Kenji about what had happened. But he wasn't there—not that day or the day after. When I asked the teacher, she said something about a planned absence. Usually, that meant someone was going on a vacation.

Kenji hadn't told me about a vacation, and when I tried to call him at home, no one answered. Remember, these were the days before cell phones. If you weren't at home, you weren't getting the call.

Perhaps they'd gone to visit family in Japan. Maybe it was a funeral.

Death. All I could think about was death.

My death.

Larry's death.

My parents' death.

Morbid? Yes.

An obsession? Definitely.

A ten-year-old has no business thinking about death day after day. I knew that, and I tried to ignore the thoughts. They kept coming. I'd see a car passing by the school bus, and I would think that it might be the last time I'd ever see that man driving to work because he was probably going to get hit head-on and die. We'd have a lesson in school about the Civil War, and the only details I could focus on were how many soldiers died in each battle.

Death surrounded me, strangled me at night, twisting and turning in my dream state, always reaching.

THE GOOD NEWS came on Thursday. I'd stepped off the bus when I saw a familiar form walk around our house.

"Carlisle!" I almost screamed it, so grateful for someone to talk to. It had been five days since Kenji had left.

"Hey, Jimmy."

He looked good. Not perfect, but a lot better than before. Like he'd had a few days of rest in a comfy place.

"James," said Mom. I swung around to see her standing on the porch with a rolled-up magazine, tapping it in her palm like a nightstick.

"I'll get my homework done, Mom."

"That's good. I also need you to watch your brother."

"But, Mom—"

"James, if you want to eat something besides rice and beans, I need to go to the store."

Larry came bounding from the house like a puppy off a leash. Mom went back into the house to get ready to leave.

"Come with me," Carlisle said with a wink in his voice.

We followed him to the greenhouse where he set my little brother to building his very own fort in one of the greenhouse beds.

"Where'd all the plants go?" Larry asked, already making mounds of dirt with his hands.

"It was time to turn the soil and get ready for next season."

Larry didn't have any response to that. Happy with his army men and dirt, we left him to his task.

Carlisle and I went to his office. I filled him in as quickly as I could, making sure to include Bruce's enigmatic statement about "the plan. "

Carlisle sat and listened quietly, nodding. He was back. Calm and ready for whatever trouble lay ahead. It made me feel ready too. Up until that very moment, I'd been a bundle of jangled nerves.

I needed a big chug of water after I finished. Carlisle let me swig from the hose. It was all I could do not to swallow the nozzle whole.

"What do you think?" I asked, panting after my long drink. "Do you think he'll tell Dad?"

He rocked back in his seat and thought for a moment, breathing heavily from his nose. I felt like he should have a pipe to puff on, like some wise old professor.

"No," he said finally. "Don't you go telling nobody—no sense in complicating things. But I'm worried about this plan of his. What's behind it?"

"And why did he let me go?"

Carlisle chuckled. "That one's easy. Too many witnesses. Me. My friends. If anything had happened to you, we'd all know who was responsible. Hell, I'll bet he was driving like an old granny on the way home to avoid any chance of an accident. If there is anything Brady Bruce cares about more than his own tail, I'd like to see it. No, he wouldn't take that kind of chance."

"So, what do we do?"

He smiled at me. "I'll think of something. I promise." Then he leaned in. "By the way, I'm proud of you."

I hung my head. "What for?"

"You stood up to him."

I didn't have a choice, but I think I understood what he meant.

"I peed myself," I said, the shame eating me up. I had to say it. I didn't deserve the praise Carlisle was giving me. I needed to knock it down a few notches.

I had expected Carlisle to throw his head back and laugh. He didn't. I felt him staring.

"Look at me, Jimmy," he said solemnly.

I couldn't bear to look up. Carlisle repeated the order. With my chin on my chest, I turned my pupils to him.

His face was as stern as I'd ever seen it. "You did what any *man* woulda done in the same situation. Now how does *that* feel?"

CHAPTER FIFTY-FOUR

"Come on, Larry," I impatiently said as we trudged home. He liked to dawdle. Anything to lengthen the time he had with me, but I wasn't in the mood. Carlisle said he'd come up with something. I wanted that something now.

Larry picked up a rock and turned it over and over in his palm.

"Look, Jimmy."

"It's just a rock."

"No, it isn't. Maybe there's a diamond inside."

"No diamonds around here."

"You don't know everything there is to know."

"Yes, I do."

That stopped him dead in his tracks, hands on his hips.

"Take your hands off your hips," I said. "You look like you're in a bikini contest."

"I'm telling Mom you're mean to me."

"Go ahead and tell her."

"I will!"

I exhaled my frustration. The adrenaline rush of my meeting with Carlisle was blowing away like an untied balloon. I bent down to look him in the eye. "I'm sorry. Can you hurry up? I'm hungry."

He grinned and grabbed my hand. As much as I was not in the mood for his shenanigans, I was equally not in the mood for the whole loving big brother thing.

We'd rounded the house when a new station wagon pulled down the drive.

Denny Bell stuck his head out the window. "Hey, boys!"

"Hello, Mr. Bell."

"How many times do I have to tell you, Jimmy? It's Denny. Remember?"

There was nothing but airy kindness in his tone. I saw a figure shifting in the passenger seat, and it was Mrs. Bell. It looked like she was asleep. Denny cast her a look of concern, as if for my benefit.

"Mrs. Bell isn't feeling too hot. Baby's coming soon. Anyway, better get going. You boys have a good night."

"Byyyye, Dennyyyy," Larry sang.

I watched the station wagon drive off. Paper tags. New car. Cool. I wanted a new car. I bet Denny's air conditioning worked. Not like ours, always blowing hot air on the days that we needed arctic cold, not to mention the radio station tuned to staticky boredom.

Larry was distracted again. I was about to tell him to hurry up when something caught my eye. A solitary figure. Upon the wall. My body turned to ice.

I grabbed Larry's hand and ran the rest of the way home.

CHAPTER FIFTY-FIVE

"No!"

Blackness consumed me. I tried to gulp in air as I twisted and turned.

It took me a minute to come out of it.

Fourth nightmare of the night.

Apparently, Mom thought two nightmares was enough. She hadn't come in the third time either. Maybe I wasn't screaming as loudly.

I spent the rest of the early morning staring up at the ceiling, imagining.

Brady Bruce watching me.

Brady Bruce following me.

Brady Bruce killing me.

By the time the sun peeked through my curtains, I was half-convinced that Bruce would be waiting for me in the bathroom.

No Bruce in the bathroom.

It was terrible having the bastard in my head. At least if he was physically there, I could shut out the sight of him by closing my eyes.

I managed to get through the rest of the night without another nightmare. I successfully programmed myself to dream about riding Marauder into battle, flanked by an army and destroying Brady Bruce, the despotic ruler of *Bruceland*, once and for all.

THAT MORNING, Kenji still wasn't at school. When I again asked my teacher, she gave me a look that said, "Don't ask me again because I don't know, and I don't get paid enough to find out."

The day dragged on, and I lugged my way with it. I ate lunch alone now. That's hard to do when the cafeteria is packed, but I found a way. No eye contacts. No words. The others got the idea. They let me be. I've since heard that it's the same with new prisoners. Inside every man is the body language of self-imposed loneliness waiting to be employed for survival.

WE'D JUST GOTTEN BACK to the classroom when the counselor poked her curly head inside the door jamb.

"May I have James Allen, please?"

The teacher waved me to follow.

I figured it had something to do with my behavior. I wasn't playing the game. I was a loner now, an outcast, stamped "defective."

"Bring your things, please, Mr. Allen," the counselor said.

I ignored the stares. They probably thought I was being committed. The crazy kid finally gets carted-off to the looney bin.

I followed her clickety-clack heels down the hallway, ignored by the counselor.

When we got to the office, the principal was there. He was a beanpole of a man with legs like yardsticks in slacks.

"James, your mother is on the way."

"Am I in trouble?"

"No. You're not in trouble."

"Then why am I going home?"

"Your mother is coming to pick you up. She'll explain when she gets here."

These masters of public relations plopped me onto a stool in a corner without further explanation. I watched the clock's minute hand click from space to space. I'd never noticed how thick the black lines on a clock were.

It took Mom a good thirty minutes to arrive. When she did, she looked a mess. Her customary makeup was nowhere in sight, and her eyes, rimmed in red.

"Oh, James," she said, rushing in to hug me.

"What is it, Mom?" I was feeling that panicky feeling now. I'd convinced myself that there was a problem at the prison. Maybe an escape. Dad liked to get us all together when that happened. Surround us with guards, and we were okay.

But Mom never cried at a prison break.

She pulled me to my feet. "I'll tell you in the car."

CHAPTER FIFTY-SIX

"James, Kenji is sick," she said and bit her bottom lip while she drove.

"Okay," I said.

She looked at me in the rearview. "It's not good."

"Okay," I repeated.

Again, the rearview look. "Do you know why I picked you up from school?"

I shrugged.

She made a noise of quiet frustration and drummed on the steering wheel for a moment, Then, Mom pulled the car over and put it in park. She leaned her arm over the seat and looked me in the eye. "Schools don't normally let you go home when your friend is just plain sick, right? You know that."

Now the realization began. My death dreams came back in a rush.

"Is he . . . going to die?"

For a long moment, Mom didn't move a muscle. I saw her eyes welling up, and her upper lip disappeared. "I'm so sorry, James. He's such a nice boy."

I buried my face in my hands and let it all go.

Somehow, Mom was suddenly at my side, pulling me into her.

All my frustration, sadness, and regret came out.

My friend . . .

CHAPTER FIFTY-SEVEN

The smell of antiseptic and sickness slapped me in the face as soon as we stepped through the front doors of the hospital. I wanted to bolt from the place.

Kenji was sitting up in bed when we got to his room. He looked like a thin piece of paper.

"Hey, Jimmy," he whispered, his voice nasal from the tube in his nose.

His mother and father stood in the corner politely staring like I was supposed to say something.

"How do you feel?" I asked, realizing how stupid the words were as soon as they came out.

He shrugged. "The forest vampires got me before I could wield my enchanted stake. How's school?"

"Full of forest vampires."

"Mom, Dad," Kenji said weakly, "could you give Jimmy and me a couple of minutes?"

Mom smiled at Kenji's parents. "Big important things to discuss. Can I treat you to some coffee?"

"That would be wonderful," said Kenji's father. He said it like it was the answer to his prayers.

I stood there awkwardly for a good minute.

"You can come closer. I'm not contagious," Kenji said.

I came closer. The beeping machine was like an ice pick tapping on my head. I held off the cringe when I saw the tubes snaking from beneath the covers.

"Does that hurt?"

"No."

"What are they?"

"Soul suckers. They're draining my soul. I'll need a spell to get rid of them."

"What happened to you? What do you have?"

"It's called leukemia. I've had it for a while."

"You never told me you had it."

"Sorry."

"It's okay," I said.

"I should've told you."

"I said it's okay."

"Please don't be mad, Jimmy."

He grabbed my hand. I couldn't look at him.

"I'm not mad," I said in frustration. Before I could realize what was happening inside me, the tears came. My breath hitched.

"Look at me, Jimmy."

I was ashamed to look. I wanted to shake Kenji's boney little hand off from mine and bury myself under a rock somewhere. When I finally looked up, I saw the opposite of what I expected. He was calm. Just like Carlisle. Serene. Ready for anything.

"I'm almost out of hit points," he said.

CHAPTER FIFTY-EIGHT

Kenji died on a Saturday. I remember because I was watching G.I. Joe. The call came first. There were hushed tones between Mom and Dad. They both walked into the room.

"James, we need to have a word with you," Dad said.

"Yes, sir."

I already knew. It was inevitable. No matter what Mom whispered about miracles every time on our way home from the hospital, Kenji had told me the truth that first day.

I shut the TV off and sat calmly on the couch, my hands folded in my lap like I was about to hear a sermon.

"Kenji died last night," Dad said softly.

I felt something tugging the corners of my mouth. I hated myself for it.

"It's okay to cry, son," said the warden.

I shook my head, fighting the tears.

"He went peacefully," said Mom, as if I had any idea of the significance of that. "He died in his sleep. There was no pain or anything."

The forest vampires, I thought. *I'll kill every last one of them.*

KENJI'S MOM was waiting for me on our front porch when I arrived home after school one day. It was a week after the funeral. Tears filled her eyes when I approached, and she clutched her hands before her like I was her long-lost son or something.

A brown box lay at her feet.

"Hi," I said, not knowing what else to say. At the funeral, Kenji's mom looked like she was under a spell where she couldn't speak or blink. Maybe she'd say something when they took Kenji's body back to Japan for burial. Dad mentioned something about it being a great honor. I didn't know about that. All I thought about was Kenji's coffin being stuffed into the cargo hold of an airplane and strapped into place so it wouldn't jar.

"Kenji . . ." Her accent was thick. She struggled to find the words. "He . . . give you this."

She pointed to the box.

"Thank you," I said, and I bowed the way Kenji had taught me.

Her gaze lingered on me for a long time.

"Ma'am, would you like to come inside? I can get you something to drink."

She stepped off the porch. "Goodbye, Jimmy. Thank you . . . for being friend to Kenji . . ." She put her hand to her mouth. There was agony there that needed to be let-go but would not find release any time soon.

That was the last time I ever saw her. She got in her car and drove off, leaving me with the brown box.

When the car was out of sight, I opened the box gingerly. The waterworks came again. It had been a busy week for tears.

CHAPTER FIFTY-NINE

Jimmy,

This stuff is for you. If I left it for my parents, they'd probably make a shrine out of it. We Japanese are pretty good at making shrines. Hey, that would be good for a future adventure. Pillaging treasure from a sacred shrine. I wish I could be there with you to play it.

I've never had many friends. I think you know that. You are my best friend. You showed me that I'm not as weird as everyone says. Thanks.

I wasn't sure if I was going to say the next part. But I'm dying, so I guess it doesn't matter.

Speaking of games, I know you think the thing with Bruce is a game, but look at me. Kids can die too. I don't want you to die, Jimmy, I want you to grow old and wise. I want you to do whatever you want to do in life. You're smarter than you know. You're smarter than your dad gives you credit for.

Well, that's it from me. Maybe one day we'll play the next adventure up in heaven. To tell you the truth, I'm a little scared. Not a lot. Just a little. We, Dungeon Masters, must face death with bravery, and that's what I'm going to do.

I'll be okay. I promise.

Take care of yourself, Jimmy. And don't ever forget me.

Your friend,

Kenji

CHAPTER SIXTY

You ever feel like someone left and took a bit of you with them?

I don't think Kenji intended it to feel that way.

I stared at the letter and his near-perfect penmanship. Even sick, he could write more neatly than I could entirely healthy.

The letter felt false, like it was someone pretending to be Kenji. I'd say, "Liar, show me the real Kenji." It wasn't fooling me.

But the letter was all I had left. I was scared to let it go. I thought maybe a wind would come and carry it off along with my memory of Kenji. I clutched it tightly, feeling the paper crinkle under my grip.

IT WASN'T until a week later that the import of what he'd written finally hit me. Kenji's saying that I was smart started something of a chain reaction. Whether it was the fact that I finally understood my potential, or maybe I wanted to take up where Kenji left off, I don't know. After he died, I did everything I could to get the best grades possible.

It wasn't easy at first. But like learning how to fly fish, soon it became a rhythm, a habit. My brain got used to the challenge. I like to think that I channeled a part of Kenji for that.

That's when I knew what he'd done. I'd learned about talismans on one of our D&D campaigns. Ever the crafty wizard, that letter was Kenji's talisman of great wisdom for me, and it had kicked on when he died.

I got all A's after that.

Even through the tragedy that lay ahead . . .

CHAPTER SIXTY-ONE

The days and weeks after Kenji's death were the calm before the storm.

When I wasn't studying, I was hanging out in the greenhouse with Carlisle. Sometimes Larry came and sometimes not. It didn't matter one way or another to me. I found I had a new appreciation for my little brother. It was as if death had darkened all unimportant areas of life and illuminated only the important ones.

One day, I was trying to memorize the correct order of events leading up to the American Revolution when the bat phone rang in the kitchen. That was the direct line to the prison, used only in case of emergencies.

"Warden Allen," I heard Dad say. No more from him. Then the purposeful stomping from the kitchen to the bedroom and out the front door.

I went to my parents' room. Mom was reading in bed, blue curlers in her hair.

"Mom, is everything okay?"

"Everything's fine, James."

"Are you sure?"

She looked up from her book. "Your father says it's fine so—"

The wail of the prison siren told us another story.

CHAPTER SIXTY-TWO

Three prisoners were missing. That meant lockdown.

Dad rarely wore a gun, but he wore one now. It'd been his father's and his grandfather's weapon before that.

I'd asked him once if guns ever go bad.

"Not if you take care of them," he'd said. He cleaned that weapon every week. More if he spent time on the range. He cared for it like a baby bird dropped from the nest.

The night dragged on, and I continued with my schoolwork. Lockdowns weren't frequent; nevertheless, we'd been through our fair share—no big deal. Nine point nine times out of ten, an escapee wanted to get as far from the prison proper as possible. The chance of these three coming to our house was slim to zilch. Still, it didn't stop guards with guns showing up to watch the house.

Mom put Larry to bed and checked in with me.

"How much more do you have to do?"

"Not much," I said. "Trying to get ahead."

She kissed my cheek. "Don't stay up too late, okay?"

She'd made it sound like she was going to sleep, but I knew better. She never slept when there was a prison emergency. Even though we might be safe, that didn't mean Dad was. The gun on his hip suggested the possibility that he might have to use it.

"He's okay, Mom," I said.

"I know," she said, caressing my hair. I saw the worry stamped on her face.

The American Revolution sucked me in for another hour. By the time I finished, I could barely focus on the page. Words squiggled across the white surface like eels slithering back to sea.

"No more," I said, tapping out.

I stretched all-the-way-back, leaning my chair on the back two legs.

When I opened my eyes, I saw a man in tattered prison overalls, standing in the doorway, gun in hand, staring right at me.

CHAPTER SIXTY-THREE

"I'm not gonna hurt you," the inmate softly said. He didn't have any front teeth. There was something in his other hand, and he noticed that I noticed.

"It's nothing," he said, displaying it. "Just a key."

"What's it open?"

His hand swiped across his top lip. "Doesn't matter." He looked left and right and took a step into my room. "I'm not gonna hurt you."

"You already said that."

"Right. Sorry."

I know you probably think I was bonkers-brain. A ten-year-old kid is supposed to be scared of a stranger in his house and now in his room, right? Well, yes. Anyhow, I'd been through a lot by that point. My nerves were burned to the base, cauterized from feeling real fear.

"What do you want?"

"You're Carlisle's friend."

"Yeah."

He stifled a nervous laugh. The prison siren blared again, and the inmate's eyes flicked to the window.

"I don't have long."

"What do you want?" I asked again.

"They say you're a good guy. Someone we can trust. Is that true?"

I shrugged.

"Here." He set the key on my desk and backed away, careful to show me that he meant no harm.

"What's it for?"

"I don't know."

I looked down at the thing. "Well, what am I supposed to do with it?"

There were shouts outside.

He crouched down and went to the window. "Shit. They know I'm here."

I had so many questions. Only one popped out of my mouth. "How did you get in here?"

"The others distracted the guards."

"The ones on the front porch?"

"Uh, huh."

I could see he was gearing up to run. His breaths came like a runner digging in at the starting line.

"Let me help," I said. "Are you Carlisle's friend?"

He straightened up at that. "Of course."

"Good. Then I'll help you."

Don't ask me why I said any of what I did. Don't ask what made me think that helping an escapee was anywhere within the realm of sanity. I was beyond sane.

"But you'll have to hold on while I talk to my mom first."

I went to my parents' room.

"I heard guards outside talking. They may have found the guys."

"That's a relief," she said. "Still though, no going outside."

"I won't. I'm going to bed."

I went back to my room, to the grit-covered inmate that was hiding in the shadowed corner.

"You ready?" I asked.

He nodded. I thought he might lose his nerve.

"Okay." I went to the window. Perfect timing. Two guards walked by. I raised, then tapped on the window as loud as I dared. I didn't want Mom to hear.

Both heads snapped my way.

"I saw them go that way." I pointed back toward the other houses on the reservation.

They didn't hesitate. One spoke into a walkie-talkie, and the other guard shifted his shotgun from a cradle to a ready. Then they were gone.

I looked at my inmate. "It's as easy as that."

"Thanks," he whispered, a smile was trembling at his lips.

"No problem."

He was just through the door when he turned. "There's about to be hell around here. Keep your head down, kid."

I nodded, not having any clue what he was talking about. But his tone suggested that he fully believed whatever *it* was he'd alluded to.

I heard the front door open. I had to strain to hear the inmate's footsteps creep away.

I breathed a sigh of relief.

I was suddenly thirsty as all get out. I went to the kitchen and poured myself a glass of water. Half of it was down my throat when I heard the unmistakable sound of a shotgun. Then a second boom.

I froze, blood pounding in my ears.

I heard Brady Bruce yell, "I got him!"

CHAPTER SIXTY-FOUR

The escape ended that night. All three inmates were dead. In the history of Dad's storied tenure, that had never happened. There'd been suicides and accidents. Not to mention the guy that was hiding in the trash. But three dead in an escape attempt made national news.

"You're staying home from school," Dad said when he finally came home. He was still wearing his sidearm.

"But I want to go to school. We've got a test— "

His finger pointed like a spear. "You're staying home. News vans are coming, and it's going to be at least two days before those idiots leave us alone. Till then, you're to stay put."

No sense arguing about it. Dad was in one of those moods. Dark as a snake pit.

The news vans showed up around lunch, and the mayor showed up right after that, followed by the governor. I watched the unfolding circus from my bedroom window.

Dad stood in the middle of it all, the face of the prison. Cigarette after cigarette came out and puffed their way to death. The Feds showed up too and caused a real commotion. The news people shuffled around like pecking hens.

Mom and I watched the news. Dad looked a lot older on TV.

"Unfortunately, all three inmates were killed in their escape attempt," he said, face stern. Eyes directed at the camera. "In the attempt, no civilians were harmed, and not a single inmate made it outside the prison grounds."

Dad always said that it was the town's biggest worry. Chances were slim to none that an escaped convict would do much harm in the city the prison resided. What civilians don't realize is that the worst they can expect is a stolen car and a few busted windows. Other than that, escapees want to go as far as possible and keep on moving.

"My staff is in the midst of a thorough investigation. No stone will be left unturned."

Dad went on; only I wasn't listening. "No stone left unturned." That thought tumbled down my subconscious. Would any of those stones build a path back to me?

"James."

"Yes, Mom."

"I asked if you wanted grilled cheese for lunch."

"Oh. Yes, please."

I wasn't hungry, and I wasn't thirsty. Electricity buzzed through my veins. I did not need grilled cheese and iced tea. Specific steps were required, and that included my next bone-head move.

CHAPTER SIXTY-FIVE

I finally went back to school on Wednesday. I spent it in a dizzying bout of concentration catching up on my missed lessons.

I found Carlisle speaking with my dad when the bus let me off in front of my house. The sight of Carlisle and the opportunity to tell him about the key and my plan sent my heart racing.

"How was your day?" Dad asked.

"Good," I said, trying not to sound too excited. "Lots of catching up to do."

"I'm sure you'll take care of it." That was the end of the questioning and Dad's middling concern for my wellbeing. His attention went back to Carlisle. "Are we agreed?"

"Yes, Boss."

"Okay, then. I'll let you get back to it."

Carlisle nodded to my father and threw a quick wink at me before heading off.

I went inside and unpacked my things, setting up shop on the kitchen table. I'd just cracked open the smelly history book when Dad came back in the room.

"James, I'd like to have a word with you."

"Yes, sir," I said, folding the book closed.

He took a seat opposite me and folded his hands on the table. He reeked of cigarette smoke, more so than usual. He breathed heavily through his nose as he stared at me.

"Sir?" I said, squirming.

"The night of the escape, did you see anything?"

"Did I see anything?"

"That's what I asked."

"Like what?"

He squinted at me. "Oh, anything that might've . . . disturbed you?"

"No, sir. Why?"

He leaned back in his chair and took a deep breath, letting it out slowly through his mouth. "I have this feeling."

"About what?"

Dad watched my hand running over the loose threads on the edge of the book cover. "Never mind. I'll let you get back to your homework."

He left and returned to prison. I opened my book and breathed a sigh of relief into the spine. It was near impossible to lie to my dad. It was like he had a hand that could reach into my skull to rake out the truth. Somehow, I'd eluded the claw end of it.

Homework would have to wait.

Carlisle was in the greenhouse tidying up a stack of plastic buckets.

"Hey," I said by way of greeting.

"Well, lookee here. How've you been?"

I sped past the pleasantries. "One of the inmates who escaped came to our house."

Carlisle stopped what he was doing and looked at me. "Anyone know about that?"

"I didn't tell anyone."

He looked at me for a long time. "What did the man say to you?"

I fished the key out of my pocket. "The prisoner gave me this."

Carlisle took it from my hand, turned it over twice in his, then turned his eyes to me once again. "Why didn't you give it to your dad?"

"I don't know." Then I told him everything the escapee had said.

"Sounds like Parker. A good man." He handed the key back to me. "I'm sorry if he scared you."

"He didn't scare me. He was nice."

"He was. Not much time left here."

"Then why did he try to escape?" I asked.

"No idea. That's all everyone's talking about. The three men who escaped were short-timers. They had nothing to gain."

"But what about the key?"

He shrugged. "Could be one of a million doors that thing opens."

"We have to find out what it opens." I don't know why I was so urgent at the time. I guess you could say that I felt some invisible clock ticking down, second by second, kinda like a creeping dread at a threat yet unseen. I could feel it over my shoulder but didn't know what it was. "Can you take it with you? See if you can find the door?"

Carlisle held his hands up. "Oh, no. I get searched every time I walk back to the prison. After the ruckus the other night, things are getting serious. No passes for trustees. They even have one of those wand things."

I nodded in understanding. I'd seen guards waving the wands over visitors, even the governor.

Carlisle took a sip from his tea. "How about we pray on it? I'm sure the answer will come."

I wasn't so sure. I wasn't exactly in the habit of giving anything up to God quite yet. That would soon change. And in a big way.

CHAPTER SIXTY-SIX

It became my personal mission to find the lock that belonged to the mysterious key. I tried every door in the house, nothing. I snuck the key into various cars I found parked outside the prison, and still nothing. I moved on to the other homes in the complex, over to Denny Bell's house, where I heard his toddler whining. I tried the home of the other assistant warden several houses down, the one who liked to fart and blame it on his dog, who always accompanied him—perhaps for the very purpose of absorbing blame.

I was soon out of options. The only possibility was inside the prison. Carlisle wouldn't take the key inside, not even after I pleaded and insisted that the solution lie inside the barb-topped walls.

"I don't know what good snooping around will do," he told me the day I appealed to him. He was working the soil in a pot of hydrangeas.

"Things are back to normal, though, aren't they?"

"Hell, little man," he said, smiling, turning his head to appreciate his work, "you been a warden's son too long. It ain't all about what it looks like from the outside."

"But even Brady Bruce," I said.

He looked up at me. "What about him?"

I hesitated. "Bruce's been . . . quiet."

"And how's that supposed to be a comfort?" Carlisle said with a stone face.

I had no answer.

ONE NIGHT, a phone call came during dinner.

"I have to take that," Dad said. Mom gave him a look of disapproval. She didn't like our dinners being disturbed. It was the one-time Dad would sit and be somewhat present. Dad answered the phone and quickly went around the corner. These were the days of phone cords that only reached as far as they stretched, good for twirling between fingers.

"Sure. Yes, sir. I'll be there in the morning," Dad said.

Dad came back, his face blank, and hung up the phone. He paused with his hand on it. "I forgot something at the office. I won't be gone long."

"Oh, Dean," Mom said.

Dad whipped around so fast I thought he'd keep turning. "Leave me to my business, woman!"

Everyone froze. Larry looked from Mom to Dad, lips puckering.

Mom's face went ruby red, all the way to the tips of her ears. "Go, then," she said, her voice an ice pick.

The front door slammed.

"Don't dawdle, James," Mom said. "Eat your peas before they get cold."

I thought, *What the hell is wrong with this family?*

CHAPTER SIXTY-SEVEN

My eyes flicked open when I heard the front door close. It was half-past midnight. Dad never stayed out this late. I slipped from my bed and tiptoed to the door.

The click of a lighter. The inhale of smoke.

I snuck into the hallway, around the corner, and outside the kitchen. Dad was sitting at the kitchen table, sucking and puffing. I watched him for a time, wondering what was turning in his head. I never really understood my father. He had a way of blanketing his feelings behind a mask of authority. There was nothing I could say to help him. He was a tough man. I had faith that he would win whatever battle he was fighting. Impossible to think any different. While my mother was the glue that held our home together, Dad was the immutable force that propelled the family unit forward.

Dad was reaching for another cigarette when I turned to go back to my room.

"You might as well come in, James."

You don't become a federal prison warden without having eyes on the back of your head.

"Come on then," he said, sending a fresh plume of smoke up to the brass chandelier above the table.

I stepped to the other end of the kitchen table and stood there. Dad didn't make eye contact, and that was fine with me. He let out a line of smoke like a spear, which then dissipated into a full plume. There was a hint of something else in the air. Alcohol.

"You want one?" Dad asked, tapping the cigarette.

"No."

"Suit yourself." He shifted in his seat, reaching into his pocket. His hand came back holding a slim jug filled with brown liquid. "I was your age when my father gave me my first smoke." He unscrewed the bottle top and lifted the flask to his lips. The alcohol was half-gone already. No wincing like I saw on television. I didn't know what that meant back then. "Had my first drink a year later. I suppose I'd be carted off by Social Services or paraded across the stage of the Donahue show if I were discovered giving you a taste of booze. Or a cigarette. But things used to be a lot different. Every boy I knew had an uncle who'd taken them aside and put a glass of whiskey in their hands." He took another drag, then said, "I'm going to be going away soon."

"Where are you going?"

He took another pull from the bottle. It was almost empty now. "To see my boss."

"Why?"

I knew I was treading on thin ice by questioning him. Chalk it up to recent encounters with violence and death. Perhaps I was developing a taste for it.

"Nothing you need to worry about."

"Is it about the escape?"

"It is."

In for a penny. "Are you in trouble?"

He didn't answer for a long time. "Could be." He sounded half-asleep now.

"Will we have to leave?"

"I don't know," he answered, setting the empty bottle on the table. His eyes became stony and looked like they were glassy.

I exited the room slowly. I left my dad there, staring at the table like a convicted man.

CHAPTER SIXTY-EIGHT

"They're calling him to the mast," Carlisle said, thoughtfully.

"What's that mean?"

"Oh, nothing for you to worry about."

The way he tried to brush me off boiled my blood. "Don't lie to me," I said with a growl.

Carlisle blinked. "You're right. I'm sorry, Jimmy. I have to keep reminding myself that you're not just any ten-year-old. As for your dad, I'm sure he'll be fine."

"How do you know?"

"A man like your father has a gift for coming out on top. Probably gets it from your granddaddy."

"He talked about him last night."

"Is that so?"

I mentioned the part of the conversation about cigarettes and booze.

"Huh," said Carlisle. "What else?"

"Nothing. But Dad never talks about his father."

Carlisle looked up thoughtfully from his work. "When I first arrived here, I remember we had a guard who'd transferred from a place in Topeka. Name of Jarret. He was this big, grizzly man—arms like beer barrels. I became kinda sociable with him, as friendly as you can be with a guard. He had this scar on the back of his head. I asked him about it. He said he'd confiscated dice from one of the inmates and, against his better judgment, decided to start a game with his fellow guards on the sly. An impromptu match. Ever hear that word? Impromptu?"

I shook my head.

Carlisle smiled. "Nothing bad. It means they didn't plan it. They'd snuck behind one of the washing machines, he and three others, and started throwing dice. Well, I don't have to tell a warden's boy about how that's against the rules, right?"

I nodded.

"Well, it so happens that your granddaddy was giving a tour of the place to some inspectors that had shown up. It was an *impromptu* visit, understand? They caught Jarret and his fellow guards. Your granddaddy was about to lay waste to all four of them. Then Jarret makes a speech. This was the stuff of legend. They say he was like . . . who's that Revolutionary guy you told me about—the speechmaker?"

"Patrick Henry?"

Carlisle slapped his thigh. "Yeah, yeah, that's right. Jarret was like him. Managed to convince your granddaddy that he alone was the one to blame, that it wasn't right to punish folks he'd led astray. He was the one who should suffer the consequences of all four. They say the visiting inspectors were impressed, and one of them had tears in his eyes. Your granddaddy nodded and said quietly, 'Very well, Jarret,' he says, and then he reaches into his pocket and takes out a pen and drops it on the floor. He nods to Jarret and says, 'Please.' And Jarret bends down. That's when your granddaddy turned his ring around. He wore this ring—did your daddy ever show it to you?"

I shook my head.

"One day, he will. Big old jewel right in the middle of it. Big ring. Your granddaddy had big hands. When Jarret bent over to pick up the pen, your granddaddy turned that ring around, so the big sharp jewel was facing down, and he lays his hand on the back of Jarret's head. They say the huge grizzly bear went down as if he'd been hit with a bullet. Blood poured out the back of his head. Your granddaddy says to the other guards, 'Clean up this mess boys and continues the tour with the inspectors."

I had nothing to say to this. My mouth hung open.

"You wanna know the strangest part of the story? Remember, this was Jarret himself who told me this story. He rubbed that scar and said, 'I deserved every bit of it. A good man, the warden. A good man.'"

"Why?" I said.

"Why what? Why was he a good man?" Carlisle shook his head. "Power is like that. When folks have power, folks like us naturally assume they have it for a reason. If they hurt us or use us or humiliate us, well, it would be far more disruptive to our view of the world if we suddenly thought they hadn't earned that power because they were wise. You understand?"

I didn't. "All I know," I said, "is that a man who hurts people for no reason isn't a good man."

"You're a good boy, Jimmy," said Carlisle. "You keep thinking the way you think. Don't let the Brady Bruces of the world allow you to think otherwise."

CHAPTER SIXTY-NINE

On the first night of Dad's trip, Mom made sure every door was locked. Twice.

"No one goes outside. You hear me?" Mom said when she tucked me into bed.

"Yes, Ma'am."

"Good." She kissed me on the forehead.

With the mystery of the key, Dad's sudden departure, and my schoolwork, my brain was overflowing. No chance I was going to sleep anytime soon. I clicked on my reading light and grabbed one of the D&D manuals Kenji had left. I flipped through slowly, marveling at the pictures and reading each of Kenji's handwritten notes in the margins.

I was halfway through when I heard what sounded like the mewling of a cat. Long and drawn out. Then it came again. It wasn't a cat.

I went to the window. There it was again.

A patrol truck drowned out the sound as it trundled by. Then I heard it again. It was coming from the Bells' house. Had to be, no lights on next door.

I thought about going to tell Mom. That thought evaporated with the heat of an idea—an adventure opportunity. My nerves had received a booster shot by pictures of paladins vanquishing writhing monsters with gleaming bastard swords.

I slipped into a pair of jeans and a sweatshirt. My shoes were at the front door. I made it there without incident and was sliding the first shoe on when I heard a squeak from the kitchen. The light above the stove flicked on, and I saw Mom filling a glass with water. I stood, frozen, waiting. She could turn my way. But she didn't, she went the other way.

With the glass filled, the light went out again and Mom went back to her room. I breathed a sigh of relief. She very well might've tanned my backside if she'd seen me.

Thankfully, the front door was creak-free. I was outside without a sound, padding my way around to where I thought the cacophony was coming from. I paused every few steps and cocked my ear. The noise kept coming—definitely not an animal, though something *like* it. My skin pricked up at the idea. My heart thumped in my throat, but I kept on.

It was coming from the Bells' house for sure.

Still no lights on. I wondered if Denny had bought his kid a dog. Could a dog make that kind of sound? No, it had to be the kid. I kept going. The strange sound was, for sure, coming from Denny's house. I should have let it be. I didn't.

And so, before I knew it, I was standing under one of the Bells' windows. The mewling was inside it. I took a chance. Standing on the tips of my toes underneath a window, I looked inside. What I saw froze me to the spot.

I was so consumed with the performance inside that I didn't notice the specter descending upon me from behind.

CHAPTER SEVENTY

Kids are quick.

Today, with my middle-aged bones and faulty vision, and my reaction time diminished to that of a sloth, I would've been a goner. But back then, I needed only the faintest movement of a shadow or the whoosh of air to stir behind me. Therefore, I did what any good spy would do. I dropped to the ground and rolled to the side. Perfect timing.

I finished the roll on my feet and sprinted away. I took a glance back as I did.

Brady Bruce stood there, unmoving. He clutched his nightstick, which rested on the palm of his opposite hand and gleamed in the moonlight. His eyes pierced the darkness, sending a stab of fear into me.

On I ran and quickly realized I was going the wrong way. I chanced another look back. Bruce was gone.

My house was falling away by now. I fell into a steady rhythm, figuring I would make a long loop around the reservation out onto familiar territory. There was plenty of light cast in the clear night. I jumped over the rock outcropping and my favorite creek. Heck, I could keep this up all night.

Something about the darkness made it feel like I was running at three times my speed.

I was rounding a proud maple that had graced us with its beautiful fire plumage in the fall when I saw Bruce coming at me, matching my speed and path. Those eyes cut through the dark. It was like a cruel game of tag where only your eyes did the tagging, and Bruce was winning.

I needed a place to hide. There was plenty of night left to wait him out. He had his uniform on. He had to go back to his shift at some point.

I scanned my mental map of the land but couldn't find a single place to hunker down. I was probably passing one every few seconds; the adrenaline pumping through me gummed up all rational thought.

Bruce veered right, his arms pumping. He'd gotten closer somehow. He was fast and seemed to be getting faster. Or was I slow and getting slower?

The realization hit, I was running farther and farther from safety. The houses were out of earshot now. No one from the prison would hear me if I screamed.

Had this been Bruce's plan all along, to get me out in the middle of nowhere and kill me? Now that thought got me running, sprinting, a streak in the night.

I looked back toward Bruce, and panic took hold of my guts. He was closer than ever.

I pushed my body to the limit, past it. I wished I were Bruce's size. With longer legs, I could've outrun him. I heard his breathing, hard and labored. It came in sickening animal grunts.

Then, out of nowhere, a log I'd once used as a sniper's den in my imaginary battles with redcoats popped into view. I ran for the tree trunk and its massive knot of roots on one end. I'd jump on top and over.

That's not what happened.

My left foot planted on the first root and slipped farther to the left. I tried to compensate, the muscles in my legs struggling to right the ship. I managed a flailing that ended with a face plant into the side of the enormous mound.

Momentum gone.

Game over.

It took a moment for the air to come back to me. I pushed myself onto my back, wincing at the pain in my ankle: a bad sprain, or a break.

As a result, there was the taste of iron flooding into my mouth. The sting of some unseen cut on my lip hit a second later. I let out a moan just as that familiar shadow descended once again.

Brady Bruce stood over me, his chest heaving, hands on his hips.

He said, "Now look what you've done."

I cursed at him, feeling nothing except rage.

And then whether from shock or pain I couldn't say, but the black lines on the corners of my vision closed in like curtains.

CHAPTER SEVENTY-ONE

The first sensation I had was rocking back and forth like I was on a little wooden boat in the middle of a lake. My eyes flashed open but closed just as quickly from the pain. Oh, the pain. It was everywhere. My face. My hands. My legs.

"It's okay. You're okay."

Mom? Where was I? I wanted to ask, but all I could muster was a pitiful moan.

"I can call the doctor," a voice said.

Now I had to open my eyes. Mom was hovering over me, a gentle smile belying the look of worry in her eyes. Then, to my abject horror, I saw Brady Bruce emerge from behind her.

"Get out!" I screamed.

"Shhh," Mom said, caressing my head. "It's okay. Brady found you."

"Should I call the warden?" Bruce asked.

"No." There was heat in Mom's voice. "I can take care of James."

Now I wanted Dad there. I wanted him to throttle Bruce and drag him away in irons. No dungeon was dingy enough for that creep.

I let out a pitiful groan filled with pain and frustration.

"If that'll be all, ma'am," Bruce said, taking a step back through the door.

"Yes, thank you, Brady."

I wanted to scream again, but my gritted teeth wouldn't open.

"Goodnight, ma'am. Jimmy."

I thought I saw a glimmer of satisfaction in Bruce's eyes; however, I couldn't be sure. What I do remember is the room spinning, me leaning over the side of the bed, then spilling everything I'd ingested in the last six hours onto the floor.

And then the world went dark.

CHAPTER SEVENTY-TWO

The realization of what I'd done arrived along with the morning. Mom was sleeping in the bed next to me when I shifted to go to the bathroom. There was still a lingering smell of vomit, and my stomach lurched.

Mom continued to sleep as I crept from the room and into the bathroom. The face that greeted me in the mirror looked like he'd lasted three brutal rounds with Mike Tyson. I was a mess. Half of my face was puffed and discolored while the other sagged from the strain of the night before. No way I was going to school. No way.

My bathroom business finished, I crawled back into bed, careful not to disturb my sleeping mother. She looked so peaceful there, her chest rising and falling in a natural rhythm. I watched her until I drifted off too.

THE DOORBELL SNAPPED ME AWAKE. When I looked at the clock, it was well past nine in the morning.

"Oh, hello," I heard Mom say at the front door. Pause. Some murmuring I couldn't make out. "I'll see if he's up for it," she answered.

Mom came into my room and was fully dressed for the day, makeup and all. "Good, you're awake. Carlisle's here. He said you were going to help him with something."

"Yeah," I said wearily, "I have to help him with something."

"After what you did last night, I ought to punish you."

"I'm sorry, Mom."

"I explicitly told you not to go outside, and you disobeyed."

"I know, ma'am."

She paused, a smiled fighting its way onto her face. "You worried me, is all."

"I know," I said again, ashamed.

"But you're here, and you're alive and well. Almost well, anyway. I'm not going to punish you. At any rate, I don't think you should get out of bed. How about I set you up on the couch? You can watch television to your heart's content."

"I'll be okay." To show her I got to my feet, holding back the wince, and flapped my arms and legs around. "See. I'm fine."

Mom shook her head. "You look like a drunken man walking a tightrope."

As if I'd just remembered it, I touched my face, though not too hard. The little touch sent searing pain along my jaw and up the side of my face.

"Mom?"

"Yes?"

"I really am sorry about last night." My voice wavered, and tears stung my eyes.

"Give me a hug," she said, opening her arms. She let go with tears of her own.

She very nearly crushed me with that hug. My body wanted to scream. The pain shot down every extremity like jets of fire.

"You're alive," she said, crying. "I was so worried."

CHAPTER SEVENTY-THREE

My renewed energy from breakfast had convinced her to let me go and see Carlisle.

He was in his office, sipping from his dented mug, hat perched on his lap.

"Well, if it ain't the Prodigal Son."

"The what?"

"Never mind. Have a seat. You look like something out of a monster movie."

I slumped into the chair across from Carlisle. I wished it was a cushy recliner instead of a metal thing that dug into my back.

"I heard about last night," he said.

"You did?"

Carlisle nodded, taking another sip of the steaming tea. "Word gets around. You know that."

"But who told you?"

"A little birdie. Anyway, I wanted you to come today because, well, I was thinking about your key. I thought maybe I could take it inside, see if we might get lucky."

I perked up at that. I'd exhausted my efforts with the

mysterious key. I'd started to think that it was some random key given to me by that escapee, making me believe it was something valuable to buy my silence.

"I can go get it," I said enthusiastically.

I was halfway to the door when Carlisle said, "Hang on. I need you to do something for me."

"Sure. Anything."

I was in a conciliatory mood, considering what he'd promised. And besides, this was Carlisle. There wasn't anything he could ask me that I wouldn't do. At least that's what I thought before I heard his request.

But when he asked, I felt like he'd punched me in the stomach, and then the side, and then the side of the head. I had to grab the door jamb to keep from reeling.

"No way," I said, my voice creaking. "Please don't make me do that."

CHAPTER SEVENTY-FOUR

"You owe him a chance," Carlisle said, his face passive.

"I don't owe Brady Bruce an apology!"

"We were wrong about him, Jimmy."

Carlisle was taking crazy pills. That was the only answer. There was no way in the world that my friend, the man who'd been on the receiving end of rage from the very person he wanted me to apologize to, no way he could want this to happen. I wanted to pinch myself to see if I was asleep, but I didn't know where on my tender body I could without sending the needling pain shooting again.

"He'll be waiting for you."

"I'm not going."

"I won't make you go, Jimmy, although I'll tell you that things will be a lot better if you do."

I thought about lying to him. I'd tell Carlisle that I'd do this thing and run home instead. My shoulders slumped. My lie would come back on Carlisle somehow. They'd take a warden's son's word over an inmate's any day. I couldn't allow that. I realized how selfish that act would be. Then I remembered what he'd said about people holding power and those who follow their every word, and it became a little clearer to me.

And so, not for the first time, I put my trust in Carlisle.

I nodded toward the floor. "Okay," I said softly.

Carlisle stood and set the empty cup on his desk.

"I'm proud of you, Jimmy." He patted me on the back. "He's waiting for you by the creek. Do me a favor. After you finish, come back to see me."

Off I marched, to my doom, to do the one thing I never in a million, billion years thought I'd do.

Apologize to Brady Bruce. God help me.

CHAPTER SEVENTY-FIVE

The shakiness in my legs soon turned to a rage-infused stiffness that made me walk like a knight in plated armor.

What am I doing? I thought. This is stupid. So stupid.

And it was. The enemy was awaiting my surrender. I saw his face in my mind's eye, leering, jeering, smug satisfaction at my defeat and humiliation.

I wondered what the hell had made Carlisle come to the conclusion that Brady Bruce was worth the spit it took to apologize to him.

I focused on the pain that still radiated around my ankle. Mom had said it was a bad sprain. I'd fix my thoughts there because it grounded me—the pain. Focus on the pain, I told myself. Every jab and jolt of it was a reminder of who put it there.

There were fifty yards between us now. Bruce puffed away on a cigarette, fast, like he was racing to the finish. The smell of cigarettes was starting to get to me. I'm not sure if it was because Dad hit the pack more when things weren't going right. Like now, it was evident since he'd returned home that things weren't their normal kosher. I'm pretty sure he sucked down two to three packs a day.

There was no raised hand in greeting from Bruce. We weren't friends, so I didn't expect it. Then I was there, staring up at him, hoping that all the rage I felt was shooting from my eyes and burning a hole into him. If it was, he didn't flinch. In fact, it seemed like he didn't even see at all. His eyes were hollow pits of nothing.

He flicked the cigarette away, and the smoke dissipated. That's when I saw his eyes, rimmed in red, raw, and puffy.

Was he crying? No way.

"Thanks for coming to see me, Jimmy," he said.

He shuffled uncomfortably, one foot, then to the other, like a kid sent to the principal's office. It didn't look like he was going to keep the words coming.

Might as well push the conversation along. "Carlisle said you wanted to . . . see me?"

A loud, jarring laugh came out of his mouth. "That Carlisle, he's a real piece of work."

I was fully prepared to mount an assault in defense of my friend, even though it was that very friend who'd put me in this shit situation.

Bruce still didn't register my hostility. That gave me pause, but not much.

"I . . . I've changed, or at least I'm trying to change." The cigarette pack came out of his pocket, and he shook it, winced, then squashed it. "Damn." He stuffed the empty package back in his pocket. "I sure could use another one. Hell, I sure could use a drink. Look, Jimmy, I've done some things that I'm not proud of. A lot of things. Carlisle's helped me realize how fucked up I've been. Sorry for my language." His hands twitched as they interlaced.

Then it was like something in his throat became uncorked, and he let out a stream of words with no end. It was all I could do to stand there and take the slap of shock.

CHAPTER SEVENTY-SIX

"You've got a good dad, kid. Do you know that? My dad . . . used to . . . aw, hell." Bruce dragged his arm across his eyes and sniffled. "My dad used to wallop me quite a bit, you know? A lot of the time I didn't know I'd done anything wrong. It would be during dinner, say, and I'd be enjoying my meal, laughing with my brother, and the hand would come in from the side and smack me . . . *hard*. He did the same thing to my mother. You grow up like that . . . hell, it's not an excuse. Let's say it takes a guy some time to unlearn the lessons of his youth, you know? Shit, I don't know why I'm telling you this."

I shuffled uncomfortably. "What about Carlisle?"

"Hmm?"

"You said Carlisle's been helping you?"

"Oh, yeah. You see . . ." He licked his lips. "One time I was . . . mean to him."

He shuffled again, and I could tell it was because he was trying to speak to me using kid language.

"I was mean to him. I liked doing it, you know? It made me feel good because I . . . I kind of hate myself. And when I could be mean to someone, it made me feel like I was right for hating myself. It's hard to explain. Do you understand?"

"I think so."

"I hate myself because my dad made me feel worthless. At least that's what my brain tells me." He stared at the ground, chewing his bottom lip. "Anyway, one time, I was being mean to Carlisle, and I did something I never did to him before."

My hands automatically balled into tight fists.

"I . . ." he continued, "I looked into his eyes, *really looked into them*. I saw how we're both humans—brothers under the skin and all that. I'd never had that feeling before with anyone I was . . . mean to."

I nodded, processing.

He held out his hand, palm down. "See this? Can't even hold my hand still." He clenched the hand into a fist and shoved it into his pocket. "I have to go, but I didn't want to leave without saying sorry. I'm sorry, kid, for everything. You got caught in the middle. It wasn't your fault. I take responsibility . . . for *everything* I did. Tell the warden if you want. I won't lie. I'll admit to it. I promise."

He put two fists to his eyes, like a little boy. "I thought maybe you could find it in your heart not to tell, to forgive me. I'll change. I am changing."

I was too dumbstruck to respond. I wasn't going to hug the guy or anything. Even a lion can play possum if he wants to. But here was this lousy bad guy begging me to believe his contrition. How could I not give pause?

An idea bubbled from somewhere inside me.

"The escape."

Bruce looked up, recognition in his red-rimmed eyes.

"Why did it happen?"

He shook his head. I saw the lie coming. Old habits don't scare away in a day. "I don't know. Just some crazy inmates."

"Don't call them that!"

He dropped his chin to his chest, chastised.

"It was your idea, wasn't it? You made them do it."

He covered his face with his hands. "I might have made them do it. But it wasn't my idea. I promise."

He was making a lot of promises.

"You're a liar," I said. There was this strange vacillation of emotion inside me. Pity gave way to compassion, which gave way to resentment, then anger. I couldn't keep track of, or a firm hold of any of them.

The hands came down, and he nodded stupidly. "I am. I'm a world-class fucking liar. I've done a lot that I'm not proud of. In spite of all I've said and done; I swear kid, it wasn't my idea."

"Then whose idea was it?"

He shook his head, so vehemently I thought his neck might snap. "No. I can't say anything. He'll kill me."

A dead calm spread through me. "Who?"

"I can't."

"Tell me *who*."

Holy cow, how his eyes bulged. "No, kid. I can't. I swear, I can't. I'm sorry."

Bruce grabbed my hands. His were ice slab cold and rough as cheese rinds. I tried to pull away, but he had me vise-like. His putrid breath assaulted my nose, and I started to panic.

"Look, Jimmy, your dad's a good guy. A good boss. Best warden I ever worked for. He's fair, and he gives a shit. Because of that, you have to tell him to get the hell out of here."

"Why?"

"Convince him to leave, that's all. Come up with something. Maybe Carlisle can help. He's a smart cookie." He chuckled at that. "Can't say I'd ever said that about a con. But talk to him. He'll know what to do. I really am sorry, kid. I mean it. Can you forgive me? Please?"

I can't properly explain what I saw in his face. The pleading. The shell he'd become.

The vacillation of emotion occurred once again, shifting me along its confusing spectrum.

"Okay," I said. "By the way, I'm sorry too."

CHAPTER SEVENTY-SEVEN

Carlisle was in the same spot I'd left him, sipping a fresh cup of tea, as if nothing of consequence had happened. The *me* of minutes ago might have yelled at him.

"Is he gone?"

I nodded.

"Did you apologize?"

Another nod.

"I'm proud of you, Jimmy. You won't know this until you're older, but one of the hardest things an adult can do is apologize. Wars have started for that."

He pointed at a seat. I refused.

"What's wrong with him, Carlisle?"

"He's an alcoholic."

"Like you?"

"Kind of."

"And you're going to help him?"

"As much as I can."

"Why?"

"Because when a man asks for help, you help him."

"Still, he's a bad man. He's evil."

"Evil is what a man *does*, not what a man is. Anyway, that's not for me to decide, Jimmy. I'm just a man. All I know is that he made bad choices, choices that helped him feel better about himself, if only for a short time. The way we think about ourselves is stronger than anything. It cuts through falsehood. It eats at you until you can do nothing but evil."

"He said Dad's in trouble."

"Right."

"What kind of trouble?"

"Listen, Jimmy. Some things can't be spoken of aloud. You have to find out for yourself. I'll help you when I can."

"So, what do I do next?"

"I think the answer would be obvious to a gumshoe like yourself."

I had no idea what he was talking about. I was just a kid. As if I didn't have enough to think about: I'd lost my best friend, I'd run face-first into a tree, and I'd seen something terrible. How could I have the answer to anything? I was a pawn on a chessboard.

Then it hit—the first clue.

The key. We had to find out what door that key opened.

CHAPTER SEVENTY-EIGHT

Carlisle and I agreed that no one in prison should know what we were trying to do. Especially not, Dad.

"He's got enough on his plate," Carlisle said. "Can you keep the secret?"

"Of course."

"You swear?"

"Pinky swear."

He gave me a funny look. "What's a pinky swear?"

I showed him. My display elicited a chuckle.

"Okay. Pinky swear." He mimicked my demonstration, and we both grinned. The search was on.

DAYS WENT by without a lick of luck. I kept my mouth shut and Carlisle snooped around the prison. Each day he'd give me a thorough rundown of where he'd searched.

"Never realized there were so many doors in the place," he said one day while going over a garden ledger. He was deep into planning the upcoming seeding schedule. He had grand plans to grow giant watermelons. "It's like now that I'm looking for doors and locks, they're everywhere."

"I went on a quest with Kenji once in our D&D game. We went searching for treasure and had to go into this dark cave filled with giant spiders."

Carlisle shuddered. "Sounds nasty."

I laughed. Then the memory of my friend took hold of my breath. Carlisle noticed.

"Y'okay?"

"Do you think he's an angel?"

"Kenji? I know he is," Carlisle answered without a shred of hesitation.

"How do you know?"

"I just do."

"That doesn't make any sense."

Carlisle looked up from his ledger. "Why doesn't it make sense?"

"Have you ever seen an angel?"

"No."

"Have you ever heard an angel?"

"No."

"Then how do you know they exist?"

That natural smile spread from his lips to the crooks of his eyes. "I have faith."

That's all he said. He didn't explain. He didn't extoll the benefits of believing or not. He said it in a way that made it final, like when you say something is black or white. It just is.

I wanted that faith. I just didn't know how to get it.

CHAPTER SEVENTY-NINE

One night, Denny Bell came over for dinner. It was a welcome distraction. I didn't usually like guests. Mom would make a fuss and make me put on a button-down shirt, but I didn't mind doing that for Denny.

"Hey, champ," he said, offering a high five.

I met his hand mid-air.

"Ouch!" he shook his hand comically. "Woah! You been lifting weights?"

"Nah." I puffed my chest out. Denny was one of those adults that made you feel good about yourself. My admiration for him had only grown since meeting him for the first time.

He always waved when he drove by or stopped to say a few words. Denny knew what to say. Always.

"So, what's cookin'? You make me a T-bone steak with mashed potatoes?" He licked his lips in anticipation. It made me feel bad for not lifting a finger to help Mom in the kitchen.

"Not this time," I replied sheepishly.

He grinned that movie star grin and then followed me inside.

Dinner was a lopsided conversation. Dad brought up work a few times; however, Denny deftly steered it back to something more mundane, whether it be the outlook for the upcoming Super Bowl or the chance of snow in the coming days. Dad took it in stride. I could tell that he liked Denny too. Or maybe he was distracted. Probably both.

When dinner was over, and we had licked the remnant of dessert from our plates (Mom made a killer cherry pie), we kids were told to leave the table and play until bedtime.

"Thanks again for dinner, champ," Denny said, hand poised for another high five.

I slapped his hand, noting the distant look in Dad's face as I passed. "See you around, Denny."

"You got it."

"What about me?" Larry asked, jumping up and down for the same treatment.

Denny held up a hand, and Larry slapped it with glee.

"Yikes! Another strong Allen man," Denny said, shaking his hand as if he'd high-fived a giant.

Larry giggled and ran from the room.

As I left the room, all I could think of was how it was possible to have seen what I had through Denny's window, and how that correlated with the awesome guy I was leaving at the dinner table. It didn't make sense. Then again, at the time, nothing made much sense.

CHAPTER EIGHTY

Mom helped Larry brush his teeth while I slipped into my pajamas. Then we switched, and I closed the door to the bathroom.

"Don't lock the door, James."

"Yes, Ma'am."

There was no need to lock the door, but I was ten. I needed my privacy. Larry had a bad habit of barging in on me when I was doing my business.

I closed the door, grabbed some dental floss, and went to work. I was getting to my second molars when Dad's voice came through the air vent.

"You need to keep an eye on them," Dad said.

"Not a problem, Warden," Denny replied.

"I don't like the look of this, but I don't have a say in the matter right now."

"I'm sure it's just a precaution."

I bent down so I could hear every word.

"We need to get this place ship-shape before the month is out," Dad said with characteristic authority. You know, I could swear I detected a little bit of something I wasn't used to hearing from the stalwart warden: *fear*.

"We'll get things right back to where—"

The next words were drowned out by knocks on the bathroom door.

"Hurry up, James. You don't want to miss storytime."

"Coming!" I hurried to finished flossing and then brushing, all the while wondering what it was that had my father so stressed.

Come to think of it; he hadn't been the same since that night with the bottle.

CHAPTER EIGHTY-ONE

I was on my way to the bus stop the next morning when I got part of the answer. A van passed by headed to the front gate of the prison. Four dour faces stared out at me—new guards, each with the look of a gallows hangman. They gave me the creeps.

I watched them unload at the gate and check-in with the guards. The guards my dad had either hired or inherited ran the gamut of size and appearance, from a six-foot-seven giant to a beanpole farmer who looked like he might fall over when he farted. The old guards were black, white, or in-between. They had one thing in common, with very few exceptions: they were good men. They were Dad's men.

These new guards were different. There was a hardness there that radiated cruelty. Perhaps it was my imagination, and the instances of that terrible year had colored my vision. But I was beyond such cool rationalizations. I saw what I saw, and it frightened me.

Two of them seemed to make a special effort to find me as I found my seat on the bus, and stare at me as we cruised away from the prison.

CHAPTER EIGHTY-TWO

Dad was in a foul mood when he came home that night, chain-smoking like a man on death row, scowling at every one of us. Even Larry, who was typically oblivious to such things, gave my father a wide berth.

"I'm not hungry," Dad announced after Mom had set the rest of dinner on the table.

She made a face only I could see and said, "I'll leave you a plate in the fridge."

Dad grumbled something and disappeared to the living room where he puffed away like a runaway train.

"Is Daddy okay?" Larry whispered.

"He's fine," Mom said. "James, why don't you say grace."

I was too curious to groan.

The three remaining Allens clasped hands.

"Lord," I began, "thank you for this food, and thank you for family . . ."

I'm not sure how I finished the prayer, because only half my brain thought about what I was saying. The other half couldn't get away from the fact that Dad was worried. As worried as I'd ever seen him. And that made me worry. And wonder.

He reappeared after dinner; a bit lighter in his mood.

"How's about you and I have a chat?" he said, clapping me on the back.

I went to my room with Dad on my heels and took a seat on my bed. Dad pulled up the chair from my desk and placed it methodically in front of me. Then he went to the door and closed it slowly and quietly.

"James, can we talk man to man?"

"Sure, Dad."

He shook out a cigarette from his omnipresent pack, then made a frustrated face as he realized where he was. Mom had a hard and fast rule about not smoking in bedrooms, primarily mine and Larry's. He held the cig in his hand, rolling it between his fingers nervously.

"It's okay," I said, meaning the smokes.

He looked at me then, not like his son, but I liked to think like a man. A peer. A cocked and wry grin. "Nah. Your mother would kill me. Then bring me back to life so she could kill me again."

We both laughed at this. It was forced. My stomach was tight.

"I know I haven't been here . . . for you," he said as he scratched his stubbly chin. I had only just now noticed it. The man was always clean-shaven as if his facial hair didn't grow at all. "I . . . what I'm trying to say is . . . I'm sorry."

I sat and waited for him to continue. Seconds were ticking by along with my thumpin' heart.

"James," he finally continued, "I've never let work affect what happens in this house. You probably don't think that, nonetheless, I haven't. You should see some wardens. Hell, I've canned more guards for wife-beating than prisoner-beating." He rolled the cigarette from one finger to another, like a magic trick. "I don't want you to think that I don't care. Your granddaddy, well, he never gave me the time of day until I was twenty-one. We shared a beer together, and that was that. I was a man, and he was a man. That was it." I could almost imagine my father and granddad, sitting on some long-forgotten front porch, sipping warm beer, and not saying a word. The Allen men were not known for their verbosity.

"I know you care, Dad," I said suddenly.

"You do?"

"Sure."

"Hmm."

He put the cigarette in his mouth, lit it, and took a drag so long I thought every pore of his body might expel smoke when he was done.

"Dad, is everything okay?"

He didn't immediately answer. He stared at the window for a long time. Then, when I thought he was going to answer, he stood instead. "Get some sleep, James."

And he left. No explanation. No 'goodnight, son.'

His exit was anticlimactic, leaving me with even more questions that I couldn't ask.

CHAPTER EIGHTY-THREE

I didn't sleep that night, but for a dream that I had. My dad stood in the center of a ring of dancing guards in the middle of the prison laundry room. Each held a black trident in his hand and wore red horns that stuck through their uniform caps. Their eyes were vertical instead of horizontal, and when they opened their mouths, a sound like the lowing of cows came out. I watched them from behind a washing machine. Then one of them turned and saw me, grinned a mouthful of yellow teeth, and came at me with the trident. I woke up just as the points touched my throat.

The dream so unnerved me that not even humming Def Leppard to myself worked to calm me down. I stared at the ceiling where the faces of those guards appeared and lingered like the afterburn splotches of a flashbulb. It was two in the morning when I finally gave up. Sweat-slick and still pondering that last conversation with Dad, I walked to the kitchen. Maybe a snack and glass of milk would do the trick.

I snatched a leftover half of a bologna sandwich and a pickle from the fridge, then poured myself a glass of milk. I took the snack into the living room. Headlights shone through the curtains. Guard patrol. Another passed by, going the same way. Late night party, I thought.

I'd finished my sandwich and half of the milk when the third set of headlights flashed by.

Strange.

I glanced at the clock—half-past two.

Still wired, I thought maybe some fresh air would do me some good.

I crept out the squeakless front door. I made it out with ease, slipping on my outdoor shoes on the porch. It was cold, close to freezing. I should've grabbed a coat.

Another set of headlights showed up from the prison, probably the front gate. I hid behind my cabin fort and watched the sedan roll by. It was one of the new guards. Had to be. He was in uniform; one arm draped out the window despite the chill.

When the car passed, I snuck around the side of the house and watched as the taillights passed the Bell's house. Why were these cars traveling in a slow succession heading out to the fields? My fields. But why? There was no way I was going to pass this opportunity up. Could this be the answer to all the riddles? By morning I'd have the clues in my pockets, and the guilty parties would be mine. At least that's what I saw in my head.

Off I went, somehow keeping pace with the car up ahead. The guard had to be careful because there were night-hidden holes everywhere. He wasn't taking any chances. Lucky me.

I knew which areas to avoid. Even with the moon at only a sliver, I saw the way. Days upon days of running and traipsing over the miles had my legs ready for the trudge. Not only that, I probably could've done the run blindfolded.

The car went over a slight rise in the road and then disappeared. When I hit the higher ground, I saw the taillights again. No other light in the direction the car was going.

I did the navigation in my head. There wasn't anything out this way, only patches of trees here and there. No buildings. No nothing.

I jogged on, now glad that I hadn't worn a coat. It was easy to keep pace and watch for hidden logs and ankle-deep streams.

I was getting a stitch in my side when the taillights went red. Then white. Then they were gone. No more than a hundred yards ahead. Time to be extra careful.

Taking a circuitous route to my destination, it took a good five minutes to see where the car had settled. There were four more rectangular shadows. I thought they might be the cars I'd seen drive-by earlier.

I was in a crouch now, creeping forward in what I figured was an appropriately spy-like pace.

A car door closed.

Closer now. Twenty yards away. Red lights arrayed in a group; all were pointing at the ground.

"Took you long enough," a voice said.

"That fucking Warden."

"I'll bet you were yankin' it," another voice piped in.

"Fuck you."

"Watch your damn mouth," said the first voice.

I was ten yards away and counted five men. I couldn't see their faces and could barely make out their shapes. They had to be the new guards.

"Everyone knows the plan, right?" asked first voice.

"Jeez. You have us come way out here to ask us that?"

There was a snicker from the group. Then the telltale rack of a shotgun.

"What, you gonna shoot me with that?"

"Not now, but I will once this is over if you don't shut your mouth and listen."

"Can we get this done? I'm beat."

"Yeah, that warden is running my ass hard," another man said.

"Holy hell, what a bunch of sissies," said first voice. "Twenty-four hours. You can't put up with it for another twenty-four hours without bitching?"

Twenty-four hours. Until what?

"If we ain't bitchin'—"

"Enough," said the first man. "Get the bags."

There was a rattle of keys, and a car door slammed. I took the chance to move left to a copse of trees I'd once hidden behind for an hour as Larry looked for me. When I settled in the hiding spot, I looked out. There'd been no trying to hush the noise. Nobody would hear them out here anyway, just me.

Yet, when my eyes trained on where they'd been, there was only blackness. No shadows. No red lights. Not even the flick of a lighter. Nothing.

Maybe they were sitting in their cars.

I waited. No more lights. No more sound.

Impossible. There was nowhere else to go. I guessed that the guards could've snuck off another way, but where? And why?

I had to know. The vehicles were still sitting in the open, and they were my chance. Maybe there was a clue.

I sat for an extra minute, listening to the leafless branches overhead clicking together like a skinny skeleton tapping its fingers. Once the coast was clear, I stepped around the tree.

I got one step. My other foot never followed.

A hand clamped down over my mouth and dragged me backward.

CHAPTER EIGHTY-FOUR

Roiling terror gripped me as I froze in the powerful grasp. I fully expected my head to get twisted around, my neck snapped, and my body left for buzzards to pick at in the thaw.

The twist never came. In fact, the pressure on me eased as I recognized the sweet smell coming off the man. He was large and looming.

"I'm gonna take my hand off your mouth now."

Terror turned to relief.

"Carlisle," I breathed in a rush as the hand slipped from my mouth. I turned and wrapped my arms around him.

"I'm sorry I scared you."

"It's okay," I lied.

He held me out at arm's length. "What are you doing out here, Jimmy?"

"I followed the last car."

"I saw that."

"You did?"

"I was lying right over there. Didn't know it was you."

Then the obvious question hit me. "What are YOU doing here?"

"I found it."

"Found what?"

He held out his hand, palm up. The key.

CHAPTER EIGHTY-FIVE

"You found the door!" I said.

"I did."

"And it led here?"

"It did."

"But won't they know you're gone? How will you get back?"

He pointed to where the guards had been not long before. "Gotta wait until they get back."

"I don't understand. What are those guards doing?"

"I'm not sure although I have an idea."

"What is it?"

"Don't worry about that now. You need to get home. Don't want to take any chances with your parents."

I didn't want to go home. I wanted to see where the guards had gone, see where Carlisle had slipped out of prison. I felt safe with him nearby. Something told me nothing would happen to me as long as he was with me.

"I'm staying," I said stubbornly.

"Jimmy, you have to listen to me. These men, these new guards, they're not like the ones you know. They're mean and don't give a flip if you're the warden's son. I have a feeling that if they find either one of us, they'll kill us."

That woke me up a tick. "But . . . they work for my dad. They—"

"The warden didn't hire these guards. They were forced on him."

I'd never heard of such a thing. Sure, there had been employees Dad had been stuck with in the past, but Dad always made the rules. The prison was his domain.

Before I could argue, Carlisle pulled me down to one knee and pointed to the clearing. The guards were back, making a racket as they came.

"Seems like we should have the others do this for us," a voice said.

"Yeah, we're not getting paid enough for this shit."

Mr. First Voice didn't try to quell the dissent this time. Maybe it was because of whatever job they were there for was done. Or perhaps he was tired of herding a bunch of misfits. I was in elementary school, and I could readily attest to that.

There were no goodbyes. Everyone climbed into their respective vehicles and took off at staggered intervals. We sat in silence until Carlisle was sure we were alone.

"You need to get home," he said.

"But I want to help."

"You have, and you will help again. I need you to do me a favor. In the morning, I need you to act like you're sick. Fake it. Stay home. Can you do that?"

"Mm-hm," I said. I'd played sick plenty of times.

"Good. Don't say anything to the warden. At least not yet. I think I have an idea of how we can stop these guys. And you're not gonna like this, but I think it's better if we let it run its course a bit, to catch the bad guys. You okay with that?"

I saw no holes in his plans, save one. "Can you get back inside?"

"Jimmy, if I couldn't, I wouldn't be here right now. I've got less than a year left in this place. I don't mean to ruin that no matter what foul plans these guards have set."

That sounded good to me. I didn't want Carlisle to get in trouble. To be honest, I didn't see the real fear at that moment. Facing mortal danger was not something my ten-year-old self was prepared for.

But it would soon be, and then some.

CHAPTER EIGHTY-SIX

I didn't have to try too hard to fake sickness the next morning. After my all-night scavenger hunt, my body needed the rest.

"Let me take your temperature," Mom said, feeling my forehead. I moaned and rolled over. "Look at this. You're soaked. Come on; let's run you a bath."

"I can't get up." I was milking it now, throwing in a grimace for good measure.

Luckily, Mom fell for it hard. "Well, okay. But if you need me, just call."

I raised a hand weakly, and it flopped back down onto my side.

"Poor baby," Mom whispered.

I watched through a crack in the curtains as Mom pulled the car out of its parking space and made its way down the long drive. She was taking Larry with her on an errand run and said she'd be back within two hours. She told me to sleep and drink fluids. I did neither.

Instead, I got dressed and went to the greenhouse. Carlisle was already there.

His clothes were disheveled, and he was scrounging around his desk when I entered.

"I'm here," I said.

He didn't say anything to me; he just muttered something to himself.

"Carlisle?"

Still nothing. Still rummaging.

"Carlisle," I said more emphatically now.

He held up a hand like you do when you've got a thought in your head that you don't want to forget. I watched him run his hand along the underside of his makeshift desk, down along the cinder block legs, inside the compartments.

"What are you looking for?"

Finally, his hand came out clutching a worn navy-blue book roughly the size of his hand. It went straight into his pocket, and he sat down with a huff. "Good," he said, wiping his forehead with the back of his arm.

"Did you find it?"

"Find what?"

"What you were looking for."

He looked at me like I'd just asked him the most insane question every imagined. Then his eyes softened, though they were red-rimmed from what I presumed was lack of sleep.

"Sorry, Jimmy. My mind's a little jumbled right now. A lot to do. And yes, yes I did find it."

He didn't explain further even though I sat there waiting. Ultimately, the silence was too much.

"Carlisle, what's going on?"

He rose and poured himself a glass of water. The first glass disappeared in one long gulp. The second went down in three. Satiated, he seemed to realize what he looked like because he started straightening his sleeves and buttoning his shirt the rest of the way.

"We don't have much time, Jimmy. It's worse than I thought."

"Carlisle!"

He paused. He looked at me. "What is it, Jimmy?"

I tried to steady my breathing as my words came out in spurts like hiccups.

"I need . . . you to tell me . . . what's going on."

He told me, and it sent tingling shivers of ice through my body and down to my toes.

CHAPTER EIGHTY-SEVEN

"So, you understand?"

I nodded. "How will these guys do it?"

"That doesn't matter. What matters is that we stop it."

What Carlisle had explained to me could've easily been a movie made for the big screen. Maybe River Phoenix would play me.

"I need to tell my dad."

"Nuh-uh. You can't tell the warden. Not now."

"Why not?"

I was no tattletale, but I'd figured that was the reason Carlisle told me everything. I never went to my dad for anything. But this . . . this had consequences for everyone.

"We'll tell him, but not right away."

I didn't think that was smart and told him so.

"Look, Jimmy, what you have to understand about your dad is that if he finds out about this, he's duty-bound to do something. Do you understand what that means?"

"Sure, that he's got to act."

"Exactly. Warden Allen's a man who believes in black or white, no gray in between. Now, if we want to make sure the bad apples get caught, we have to be careful. I have a sneaking suspicion that if the bad apples were to catch wind of us snooping, they'd just tuck tail and run. Or worse, they'll change their plans, and we won't have a shot. I've got enough friends in this place that can make it happen. I need you to stay quiet for just a bit."

There were so many reasons not to do what Carlisle said. I feared for him. I feared for me. Heck, I feared for my dad, and that wasn't something I could ever remember doing. He was *The Warden*. Prisons called him in to fix this kind of thing. Shouldn't he be responsible for fixing this mess?

"Okay. I won't tell Dad yet."

"Good. Now listen. Here's what we've gotta do . . ."

CHAPTER EIGHTY-EIGHT

Carlisle explained that the way he'd gotten out of the prison and then back again was a tunnel no one seemed to know about. Not even the longest-tenured inmates who'd been there a lot longer than Carlisle knew about it. There were few secrets within prisons walls, especially one as monumental as a possible escape route.

"I think a long time ago they used it to bring in supplies and maybe even new inmates," Carlisle said. Then he went on to explain what he thought was going on. "I couldn't find the bags, but I did find another door. It was locked. I'll bet they stashed their things in there. It's gotta be stuff they're smuggling in and out. It's the only explanation that makes sense."

This made sense to me, also. Dad said one of the things that prisons would always battle was contraband of all kinds. From drugs to nail polish, prisons had voracious appetites for legal and illegal goods alike. But this, a secret tunnel and new personnel to ramp up smuggling, that was something I'd never even heard guards whisper about.

Carlisle said he'd set things in motion from inside the prison. By the time the last bell rang, everything would be taken care of. He didn't tell me exactly how he would accomplish this feat, and I didn't ask. Better not to know some details. Because let's be honest, if things went sour, and the Feds descended on our unpretentious prison, a ten-year-old boy wouldn't survive interrogation. I held no illusion of standing up against bright lights and barking agents.

So, my job was to wait. Wait and listen.

Mom came home, and I did my best Ferris Bueller sick routine. Sick but not *too* sick. Lethargic but not *too* lethargic.

Dad came home twice, never once checking on me. I heard his voice in the living room, smelled a whiff of smoke. I thought of running in there and telling him to be careful. Still, I didn't. That wasn't the plan. The plan was to grab the bad guys and send them off to wherever bad guys went when they were too bad for Dad's prison.

So why couldn't I shake the idea that something was terribly, terribly wrong?

CHAPTER EIGHTY-NINE

The last bell sounded, and I sat up straight in bed. My sick act was slipping, and I didn't care. I needed to *do something*. Carlisle was probably organizing a rebellion inside the prison, and here I was sitting in bed, faking the Asian bird flu, or whatever and trying to read a book. Mom wouldn't let me watch television.

My mind went where it liked to go, to the worst possible scenario. Carlisle was probably chained to a wall and getting ready to spill the beans under threat of a cat o' nine tails lashing. Then they'd come after me. Or would they come after Dad first? I had to do something. But what?

My feet hit the floor, and I was out of my pajamas and into a pair of jeans and a sweatshirt. Do you know those alarm bells that clang inside your head when bad things happen? Well, those were knocking into each other like a medieval church bell.

Shoes on, I went to the kitchen where Mom was making dinner.

"Mom?"

She didn't look up from the carrots she was peeling.

"Yes, James?"

"I was thinking of going for a walk before dinner."

Now she looked up. "You go for walks now?"

"I just . . . felt like some fresh air."

"It's dark out."

"I know."

"It's cold."

"I need some fresh air."

She was going to protest, but my savior came in the most unlikely form.

"I wanna go," Larry said from the living room.

"No," I said. Larry was another complication I didn't need. I tried to come up with an excuse. "I won't be out long. And it's cold."

"I think Larry should go with you. He's been indoors all day."

"Yay!" Larry was already running for his shoes and coat.

"Come on, Mom."

"Don't you 'come on Mom' me. I wasn't going to say anything, but ever since . . . well, ever since Kenji got sick . . ."

"He died, Mom," I said quietly.

"I'm sorry. Yes. Ever since Kenji died, you've been different with your little brother."

I had, although, I wasn't going to admit it. How could I tell my mom that I felt guilty for not spending more time with Kenji? I felt guilty that he was dead, and I was alive. I felt guilty that despite knowing my lost time with my friend, I still didn't want to spend real time with my little brother.

"Okay, I'll take him," I said grudgingly.

"Good. Be back in an hour."

"I thought you said dinner was gonna be ready in thirty minutes."

"I don't see why you two can't spend a little extra time together. Be nice to Larry, okay, James?"

"Sure, Mom." Then added under my breath, "Whatever."

Larry came hobbling back, trying to zip up his winter coat. I bent down to help him.

"You're a good brother," he said.

"Who told you to say that?"

"No one."

I rolled my eyes and off we went, General Washington and his little baby brother.

CHAPTER NINETY

The winter air was revitalizing like a tonic, and I needed to clear my head. Larry was holding my hand.

We went to the greenhouse first—no Carlisle.

"Dammit," I whispered.

"Dammit," Larry repeated.

"Don't let Mom and Dad hear you say that."

"Why?"

"It's a curse word."

"What's a curse word?"

"Something that makes your parents' ears bleed when you say it."

He let out a whine. "No."

"If you don't want it to happen, then don't say it."

We went to Carlisle's tiny office. The place was clean of clues.

"What are we looking for, Jimmy?"

"Nothing."

"Where's Carlisle?"

"I don't know."

"You're looking for something."

"I know, brat. I'm looking for a book. I let Carlisle borrow it."

"What book?"

"*How to Kill Your Little Brother*."

Again, the whine. "What are you looking for?"

"Stop asking me stuff, alright?"

"Sometimes I bring Carlisle sugar," said Larry.

I looked at him. "What for?"

"For the hummingbirds."

"I didn't know that."

He nodded with solemnity like it was the most critical job in the whole world. "I put it in a napkin for him. He makes it into the red stuff and puts it in the bear bottles."

Carlisle had never once mentioned it. I'd seen the honey bear bottles, of course. He'd fashioned makeshift humming-bird feeders out of a bottle and some string. Maybe that's what Harley had been scrounging around for all those months before.

"That's really cool, Larry."

My brother's chest swelled with pride.

"Hey, listen," I said. "I need to go on a long walk, and I'm not sure you can keep up."

"I can keep up."

"It's pretty far, like over a mile. I have to run."

"I can do it."

I sighed and searched for any excuse to leave him behind. He'd be perfectly safe in the greenhouse, but unless I could produce something spectacular for him to play with, there was no way he was staying. I had work to do—lifesaving work.

"Okay. But if you get tired, I can't bring you back."

"I won't. I promise."

CHAPTER NINETY-ONE

True to his word, Larry never once complained. I had to slow my pace at times and help him around a drop or rise that was too much for his little legs. But he set his jaw sternly and chugged along for the rest of it.

We made good time. The moon seemed to be giving an extra boost of light despite its small form. Slowing as we neared, I put a finger to my lips.

"We need to be extra quiet now."

"Okay," Larry whispered back.

The tunnel entrance was just past the next rise. I strained to hear any commotion on the wind. Nothing.

"Come on," I said.

We made our way to the tree I'd used as a hiding spot before, where I'd overheard the new guards jabbering on. There were no cars this time. No guards. No secret bags.

"What are we looking for?" Larry asked.

"A tunnel."

"Really?"

"Yeah. It's right over there."

"I don't see it."

"That's because it's dark."

"What's in the tunnel?"

I'd done it now. The Larry Allen floodgates were open.

"Let's not talk about it, okay, Larry?"

"But I wanna know—"

Then, before I could tell him to keep his questions to himself, alarm sirens wailed in the distance.

CHAPTER NINETY-TWO

They went on and on for what seemed like a good ten minutes. We should've run for the house. It's easy to see that now. But then, so much of what happened next would've been stripped from history. History would be deprived of another fascinating memoir. You make decisions, good and bad, that turn the engines of fate one way or another. I made the decision to stay.

Larry squirmed next to me.

"Stop moving," I said.

"I can't help it; I need to pee."

"Then, pee."

"I need a bathroom."

"You pee outside all the time."

"Yeah, but—"

I clamped my hand over his mouth when I saw it. A flicker of movement. Right there. Right where I knew the tunnel was. I didn't exactly know where the entrance was. Carlisle said it was hidden. Not too hidden, but hidden enough to not be able to see from a distance, especially not in the dark.

Larry tugged at my wrist. He was dancing from foot to foot now.

"Go right here," I whispered.

Larry shook his head.

Just when I thought that maybe the shadow I'd seen was Carlisle, the shadow turned to two, and then three.

"Jimmy," Larry moaned through my hand.

I put my lips next to my brother's ear and said, "There are bad men over there. If you don't be quiet, they're going to hear us and hurt us."

Instead of panic, his body relaxed. I thought that was a good thing until the realization hit. Larry had peed himself.

CHAPTER NINETY-THREE

Larry started whimpering, and I nearly panicked.

"It's okay," I said, as quiet as I could. "You're okay. I'll help you change when we get home, and I won't tell Mom, okay?"

I could tell he was trying to be brave. He'd been so proud of being potty trained. I saw it in my mind's eye. Cheers from Mom. Less than enthused claps from me as Larry held his last diaper over his head in triumph.

"I'm in trouble," Larry said, sniffing so loud I was sure the guards would hear.

My body was tingling with nervous anticipation now. "What did I just say? You're not in trouble, Larry. I promise. I won't tell Mom."

"Dad?"

"I won't tell him either."

That bucked him up a couple of notches, reducing his sniffles to spasmodic sucking.

I risked a glance around the tree. The movement of shadows continued, like writhing snakes in an oily pit.

"We need to be extra quiet now. Can you do that?"

Larry nodded, adding a mouse sniffle at the end.

"Good. I promise I'll get us home safe."

It was a promise I had no business making.

I readjusted my position and said, "I need to get closer and see what they're doing. Can you stay here for a minute?"

"I can't."

"Larry," there had to be words for a time like this. "You know what? I think you're braver than me."

"I am?"

"Sure. Remember that time you went to the hospital? After the fort?"

"Yes."

"Well, you were way braver than I could've been. I swear."

His round eyes didn't look convinced. "I'm scared."

"I know you are. I am too. But you can be scared and still be brave."

I was some fount of wisdom.

"Even the toughest superheroes get scared," I said.

"Superman?"

"Even Superman."

"G.I. Joe?"

"Definitely G.I. Joe." Another glance around the trees. Less movement now. "Are you okay if I leave you?"

Please say yes.

"Yes."

"Okay," I said, letting out a breath. "Sit on the ground. I promise I'll be back in a minute."

Larry sat down and folded his hands in his lap. "Hurry, Jimmy."

"I will."

There I went, once again making promises I had no business making.

CHAPTER NINETY-FOUR

I was out from behind the tree on tiptoes, another black shadow moving towards the tunnel entrance. How many dark tunnels had been the adventures of my mind; filled with bats, giant spiders, and all kinds of unfathomable evil. The terrors of my nightmares. I had no intention of actually going into the tunnel. I just wanted to see what they were doing in there.

A man's face flashed in the moonlight, set and focused on his work. I could see the bags. Large duffels slung over a shoulder. I soon heard the grunts as the duffels were heaved on a trailer with no truck to pull it. The bed was almost full.

"Hurry up," someone whispered.

"I'm hurrying," another said.

The prison siren pierced the night air causing more than one of the hunched forms to pause.

"I said, 'hurry,'" said the man in charge.

They'd started the second layer of duffels when a beam of light cut through the dark, illuminating the working party. I tensed at the intrusion, thinking that maybe this was a search party from the prison.

My hopes were dispelled first by the lack of concern from the working party, and then by the sound of a deep truck engine coming over the ridge. I had to get down on my belly under a bit of biting scrub. The inherent dampness of the winter ground spread along my torso, making me shiver all over.

At least I could see them all now, clearly defined by the truck's beams. Just as I'd thought, there were neat rows of green duffels lining the trailer.

"Get it hitched," one of the men said.

Two men got to it without a word, guiding the truck forward and then around so it could back in and onto the hitch. With the powerful beams turned, I took the chance and went back to join Larry.

I made it back to the tree in one piece.

One problem. Larry was gone.

CHAPTER NINETY-FIVE

"*Stupid, stupid, stupid*," I said to myself.

"Jimmy," came the whisper, and I whipped my head in its direction.

"Larry?"

"Over here."

I could make out his shape some ten feet away. "What are you doing over there?"

He was hiding under a tangle of bushes, chest high. "It's better over here. You don't have to look around the tree."

He was right; you could hunker down and see the tunnel entrance, perfectly. I could even see the dim light inside.

"Good find, Larry."

I imagined him grimly nodding as I settled in on the ground next to him.

"*It's on*," one of the men at the hitch said.

Something popped in the distance. Then another. You grow up around prisons; you know the sound of gunfire when you hear it.

"It's starting," the man in charge said.

The men moved faster now with the bags. The light from

the tunnel blinked out, the only glow coming from the brake lights of the truck. Without a word, they piled into the back of the truck and eased away from the tunnel.

"What are they doing, Jimmy?"

"I don't know. But I'm gonna find out."

When I was sure the coast was clear, I helped Larry out of his hiding spot and onto his feet.

Hand in hand, the brothers Allen went to find out what this mysterious tunnel was all about.

CHAPTER NINETY-SIX

They'd left the grass-covered door ajar. That told me the men did not need to come back.

"Are we going inside?"

"No. We need to get you home."

"But I want to help."

"You did help."

I wasn't lying. The responsibility of my little brother's well-being had imbued me with an extra ounce of courage.

It took us longer to get back than to get there. Larry was huffing but still pushing as we neared the residences. The prison was lit up like a summer's day.

"Why are all the lights on?" Larry asked.

"I don't know."

"Is Dad in trouble?"

"I think he's okay," I said, not wanting to scare him.

When we got home, we found that the guards had left.

"Huh," I said, then froze to my spot. "Oh, no . . ."

"What's wrong?" Larry whined.

"*Mom.*"

I ran into the house, leaving Larry in the dust.

"Mom!" I yelled as I burst through the front door. *Oh god, the door was unlocked.* "Mom?"

No answer, all we heard was just the next siren blaring from the prison.

CHAPTER NINETY-SEVEN

"Where's Mom?" Larry had come in the front door behind me almost shocking me out of my socks.

"Jeez. You scared me. You shouldn't do that, Larry."

He cowered back a step, his lower lip kicking out in a pout.

This was no time for me to go all high horse on him. "It's okay," I said, not really meaning it. But if I didn't calm Larry down, I might be in real trouble.

"I'm scared," he said.

"It's gonna be okay."

I wrapped him in a hug and picked him up. He was feather-light.

"Where's Mom, Jimmy?" he asked with a whimper.

We both jumped when the phone rang. I gathered my guts off the floor and set Larry down.

"Hello?" I said, noticing my shaking hand as it held the receiver.

"James, where have you been?"

"Mom . . ." Everything inside me relaxed. "We're at the house."

"Well, of course, you're at the house," she barked.

"W—where are you?"

"I'm at the Bells'. I'm coming to get you."

"No!" I answered a little too quickly.

"James Allen, you listen to me right now. I've been worried sick. Your father is furious. Like he doesn't have enough on his hands."

"Mom, what's going on at the prison?"

There was a pause, and there was the sound of breathing. "Your father didn't say. Denny said it's something with the inmates."

"Is Denny with you?"

"No. Denny left to help your father." My gut twisted as Mom continued, "Pack some things. I'm coming to get you."

"Okay," I said at last.

The line went dead, and I stood with the receiver in my hand, thinking. If Dad and Denny were both gone, who could I talk to? I couldn't tell Mom about the tunnel. I wished Carlisle were there. My sage. My voice of pure reason.

"Larry, quick, change your pants, get your backpack, and put some things in it," I commanded.

"Toys?"

"Sure. Whatever you want. Stuff to do, and your blankie if you want."

Larry rushed off, and I took my time. Sure, I wanted to be safe. If Mom was at the Bells' house, there had to be guards there, also. How much time did I have?

I was thinking about what I should bring when the bat phone rang. The next ring jangled me to my toes. I crept up to the phone like it would come to life and swallow me whole. Another ring.

It's just a phone, Jimmy. Pick it up . . .

"Hello?"

"Jimmy," said Carlisle. "Thank God!"

"Carlisle?"

"I don't have time, Jimmy. Listen, your dad's in trouble. I don't know what to do."

"What's wrong with my dad?"

I heard clanging and shouting on the other end.

"You need to get help. You hear me, Jimmy?"

The racket drowned out the other end. Carlisle's voice came on again, cutting through the noise. "Do whatever you have to do, Jimmy. Get help and make sure . . ."

The phone squelched in my ear and went dead. I was staring down at it when the lights went out.

CHAPTER NINETY-EIGHT

L arry's voice came from the back of the house.
        "Jimmy?"

"I'm coming."

I found him standing in the middle of his bedroom, thumb in his mouth, blankie in his opposite hand.

"What happened?" he asked with his thumb still in his mouth.

"The lights will come on soon," I said. The power and the phone going dead couldn't be a coincidence. In my head, I did the math. The piercing sounds of the sirens had been going for close to an hour. If they'd been blaring that long, where were the reinforcements? The local police? The Feds?

"Finish packing," I said.

"I can't see."

I went to the window and flung the curtains open. The light from the moon illuminated the room.

"There. See? Better? I'll be right back."

"Don't leave," Larry whined.

"Larry, you need to be brave. Can you do that for me?"

He nodded; thumb still stuck toddler-like between his teeth.

"Good." I grabbed his backpack from the closet and handed it to him. The thumb finally came out. "Pack some things. Not too much."

I wondered why Mom hadn't come back as I packed. There were the D&D books and a random comic that'd been on my desk for months.

Carlisle had said I needed to get help. The phones were dead. How was I supposed to get help? I could run to town, but I'd have to run by the prison to get there. Whatever was going on, or whoever was running the show would undoubtedly have the road blocked. So, no running to get help.

Think, Jimmy.

I looked around the room, and my eyes settled on the Revolutionary War diorama sitting on my dresser. I had an idea.

I made a quick trip to my parents' room to the secret compartment Dad had shown me. Now packed and settled in my course, Larry and I left the house hand in hand to find Mom.

CHAPTER NINETY-NINE

She met us on the Bells' front porch and squished us in a hug. Mom answered my question before it left my mouth.

"I'm sorry, I didn't come. Mrs. Bell is having contractions."

"What's a contraction?" Larry asked.

"She's going to have a baby, honey."

"Like right now?" I blurted.

"Maybe. Come inside."

I didn't want to go inside. Images of blood, guts, and gooey babies covered in gore kept me from stepping across the threshold.

"Can I stay outside?"

"It's freezing. Don't be silly."

That's when I noticed what should've been obvious.

"Where are the guards?"

"They had to go back to prison." I knew the tone. She was trying to make it sound like it wasn't a big deal. But I heard the fear behind her voice. "Now, come on. Your brother's shaking."

I felt uncomfortable as soon as the front door closed. It could've been the eerie light cast by the pair of candles on the side table. Or the way the shadows danced on the ceiling. Or the continued siren blare. There was a smell in the house like overripe fruit, acrid, and sickly. I thought I might choke on it.

Mom and Larry didn't seem to be affected. I was going to puke.

"Can I use the bathroom?" I asked. No way she was going to let me back outside.

"Of course. But don't use hot water."

Thankfully the water was running. I double-cupped scoop after scoop of water and soaked my face.

Snap out of it.

I'm not sure whether it was the water or the item in my backpack that made me feel better, but when I left the bathroom, I felt more myself. There was a moan from what I assumed was the master bedroom, and then my mom's voice, "It's okay. Just breathe."

"What's wrong with her?" Larry asked, peeking around the corner of the living room.

"She's having a baby," I said.

A high keen wail cut through the quiet house. I froze.

"James?" said Mom. "I need you to find some towels and soak them in cold water."

"I don't know where the towels are."

"Oh, for Heaven's sake! Find them, James!" Her tone left zero room to argue.

I found a pile of hotel towels in the powder room. I also noticed how the end of the toilet paper folded to a point. *What was wrong with these people?*

I soaked the hand towels in the kitchen sink and scrounged a pot from one of the few cabinets. The house was smaller than ours but much neater. Even in the dark, it was hard to miss how every little thing had its place. I opened a drawer and saw forks piled parade-ground-neat and knives lines up like soldiers. The glass cabinet was the same. There were coffee mugs with logos that all pointed out, handles all on the right. It was like everything was for display purposes only.

Pot in hand, I trudged down the hall.

"I've got the towels," I said, not wanting to go all the way to the master bedroom.

"Bring them in."

No way. "Can you come to get them?"

"I'm a little busy, James, okay? Bring them in."

I gulped down my apprehension and prepared myself to wipe any and all details of the room from my mind as soon as it was over.

Lord, how the sweet sickly smell hit me! I almost ran from the room. However, my eyes fixed on the form laying on the bed. Mrs. Bell's face was far from her cute self. I couldn't ever look at her the same after that night. Maybe if I'd been older, it would've been different. Maybe.

Her pregnant belly moved from side to side like the little thing would burst forth at any moment. It made me think of one of Kenji's adventures. He'd led me into the prettiest meadow in the realm. I thought there'd be a cache of treasure or a flying horse for me to take as a trusted steed. Instead, there was a single egg the size of a wine barrel.

"As you near the egg," Kenji said, "it starts to pulse like something's trying to get out. What do you do?"

"I reach out and touch it."

Kenji nodded gravely. "You step forward and touch the egg. As your fingertips make contact, the egg pulses under your touch. You try to pull away, but your hand is stuck."

"Pull it away! I want to pull it away!"

"You can't. There's a crack in the side of the egg now."

"Aw, come on, Kenji. Get me out of the meadow."

"Sorry, Jimmy. This is the price you pay for curiosity. With a shriek, the egg bursts open, covering you with gobs of gore. You wipe what you can from your face only to see a baby troll leering over you, its spindly arms and legs grasping."

I'd learned my lesson. I wasn't getting anywhere near Mrs. Bell's pregnant belly.

"James, give me the towels."

Up to that point, Mrs. Bell hadn't made eye contact. Then, her head twisted to the side, and her eyes locked with mine.

"Get it out!" she shrieked.

I fell back, the pot dropping from my hands.

"James!" Mom said.

I backpedaled on hands and feet, Mrs. Bell's eyes never once breaking from mine. She pleaded with me silently, as if she could see inside me. Like she knew what I'd seen. Did she know? Had she seen me? Impossible yet possible.

Mom picked up the overturned pot and pulled out a towel.

"Now, now. You'll be fine."

I knew she was saying it to Mrs. Bell, that poor woman, but I wished she was saying it to me. The horrid sight, the terrible smell . . . I'd had enough.

"James, bring some ice from the kitchen."

I wasn't listening. I had to get out.

"Okay," I said, not knowing what I'd said okay to.

Out of the room and down the hall I went. Larry was waiting.

"Stay here. I need to get something from home," I said, trying to keep my voice calm though my brain was screaming for me to run.

"I can come."

"No."

"Why not?"

I searched for an excuse. Any excuse. Come on, Jimmy, you're good at excuses.

"Mom needs your help."

"She does?"

"Yeah, and she wants me to get you a surprise from the house." Now I was rolling. "If you stay here, I'll get it for you, okay?"

"Okay!"

A little white lie to give me a pass.

Standing outside, I breathed in repeatedly. Clean air. Pure, clear, and fresh air. My nausea subsided, and my brain snapped back to semi-normal working order.

"Carlisle," I said to the darkness. I'd forgotten about Carlisle.

I knew there was only one thing I could do. With a final look back at where I'd left Mom and Larry, I sprinted off into the night.

CHAPTER ONE HUNDRED

The tunnel's earthen door felt like it was calling me. I traced an edge with my hand, kicking myself for not bringing a flashlight. It was ebony black down there. Regardless, it was the only way in. At least the only way I could think of.

Stupid. A ten-year-old kid is running to the rescue. What else could I do? It was naive and reckless, but with the phones out and no sign of the local authorities, what were my alternatives?

"Screw it," I muttered, and took my first step into the prison proper.

The sides of the tunnel were a mix of concrete and brick. I'd imagined a dirt passage crawling with worms. Well, no creepy worms. At least not that I could see.

Not that I could see.

I tried not to let my imagination take hold. There were too many possibilities of what lie hidden in the darkness. Critters. Crooked guards. Traps. Dead bodies.

I pushed each and every image away by imagining Carlisle walking in front of me.

"Come on," he'd say. "There's nothing here that can hurt us. You know who's looking down on us."

That gave me the courage to pick up my pace and soldier on.

In my muted new world, I couldn't hear the sirens anymore.

CHAPTER ONE HUNDRED ONE

I found out I could see vague shapes there in the tarry blackness. I kept trying to tell myself that I had infrared vision like the dark elves in Kenji's stories. My dead friend's imaginary world helped me put one foot in front of the other.

The end of the tunnel came so abruptly that I all but face-planted into the door at the other end. My hand reached out and touched the cold steel. Fear gripped me again as I groped for a handle.

It took a mighty push, but the ancient portal opened, dumping a new world of sound and smell onto me. The siren blared again, seemingly miles away.

Something clanged nearby, and I flinched. Light bobbled and wavered. I got my bearings.

I was in what looked like some sort of storage room, large and full of half-empty racks.

There was a scream followed by the distant pop of gunfire.

"*Pssst...*"

I flattened my back against the wall. The contents of my backpack jammed painfully into my lower back.

"Hey, kid."

I froze, fear pounding in my neck.

"Kid?"

A form materialized from the shadows, slow, shuffling.

"Carlisle?" I asked, my voice a rasp.

"No." Followed by a strange giggle.

"Who . . . who are you?"

"Carlisle sent me."

I could see the man now. His body was slightly off-kilter like he'd been knocked left and never righted.

"What's in your backpack? Got any food?"

"Uh-uh."

There was a shrug and then another chuckle from my first prison contact.

"It's okay. Just hungry is all. The cafeteria workers haven't fed us today. Your friend Carlisle's upstairs, by the way."

Emergency lights cast themselves across his eyes. My breath caught when I saw his one dead eye, milky and unseeing.

"Ca . . . can we go see Carlisle?"

Like he'd forgotten his task, he nodded suddenly. "Look at me now. Some helper I've turned out to be. Carlisle will think I've gone off my rocker again. Wouldn't be the first time."

CHAPTER ONE HUNDRED TWO

My guide ushered me forward, murmuring to himself along the way, occasionally telling me we had to be quiet. Despite my mind and body being on the proverbial edge of reason, I couldn't help being impressed by his duality. There was no doubt that his mind wasn't all there, but somehow he knew every turn, every place we had to stop and wait to make sure the coast was clear. There was a deeper part of his mind unscarred by life. It was like some primal GPS accessed by whatever vestiges of sanity he had left.

"Almost there," he murmured. He crouched down and motioned for me to do the same. "Say, you sure you don't have any food in that bag?"

It was probably the tenth time he'd asked.

I went with my old standby. "No. Sorry."

He shrugged unconcernedly again and then looked at me as if he recognized me. "Your name Gilly?"

"No."

"Got a brother named Gilly?"

"No."

He squinted at me. "Huh. Not sure I believe you. But you're alright."

A thunderous boom shook the room, and I put my hands on top of my head for fear that the roof might cave in.

"Flashbangs, probably," the inmate said, picking his teeth with a pinky. "I wish they'd go on and get this over with. Need to get back to my job in the laundry." He giggled to himself.

Then he was up and moving again. A trio of inmates with an assortment of homemade weapons ran across the hallway. My escort didn't slow.

Voices and shouts were coming from every direction. Bangs and screams. I would have jumped straight through the ceiling if someone had tapped me on the shoulder.

"Here we are." There was a doorway up ahead. My escort gestured grandly to it. "*Entre Vous.*"

Gulping, I stepped past the door noticing that it hung off its hinges.

What I saw inside made me inhale my guts back down my throat.

CHAPTER ONE HUNDRED THREE

"You made it," Carlisle said, crouched by the body of a blood-covered guard. He stood up and shook my escort's hand. "You did good, Jo Jo. Thank you."

"All good, Carlisle. Now, I better get back to the laundry."

Carlisle put up a hand. "Don't go the usual way. Take the back way. When you get there, hide. You hear me?"

Jo Jo cocked his head to one side. The move seemed to help his brain compute, and he said, "Right. I'll get there and hide. You'll come to get me when it's done?"

"I will," answered Carlisle.

Jo Jo grinned, and then he was gone.

"Come here, Jimmy." He crouched next to the unconscious guard.

Squeamishly, I stepped closer. A crimson-soaked rag wrapped the guard's forehead.

"Is he going to live?"

"Probably, but he needs help." He stood and wiped the blood from his hands onto his pants. "Not exactly a walk in the park, is it? The trip here, I mean."

"What's happening, Carlisle?" I wanted to hug him, to make him tell me that everything was going to be okay.

He shook his head. "I was wrong. I thought it was all about smuggling."

"Smuggling what?"

"Some drugs. Some weapons. Mostly a bit of money here and there. I mean, it *is* about that, but it's not."

"Where's my dad?"

"Holed up with some guards."

"Is he okay?"

"As far as I know."

"Then, we need to help him."

"Don't you worry. The warden can take care of himself. Besides, I need your help with something else."

Carlisle told me what he needed. He described it with little or no emotion. And I knew before he finished that I was going to ignore his directions.

CHAPTER ONE HUNDRED FOUR

There was a group he described as "safe inmates" and a small cadre of guards that he wanted me to escort through the tunnel to safety.

"You get them out and take them to the greenhouse."

"Okay."

He looked at me like he saw my deception. "You sure? No questions?"

"I trust you."

"Good."

We dodged two skirmishes and one verbal battle between barricades. Along the way, we picked up a pair of inmates here and a trio of guards there. The guards were scared and still armed. I didn't ask the obvious question of why they weren't part of the fight. They didn't ask why I was there. They seemed to glaze over my presence, even when Carlisle told them I was in charge. They had the blank look of sheep without a master.

By the time we got back to the storage room and the tunnel entrance, I'd counted a total of twenty in our entourage.

Carlisle halted the procession. "Boss Hicks?"

A portly guard I recognized from the front gate turned to face Carlisle.

"Jimmy here will show you the way. You remember what we talked about?"

"Sure, sure." It didn't look like Guard Hicks was all there. His eyes shifted from left to right as if they ran on clockwork.

"The rest of you listen to me." The motley crew hushed their chatter and gave Carlisle the floor. "You go where Jimmy takes you and don't say a word, you hear me?"

There were murmurs and a couple of curses.

Carlisle put his hand on my shoulder. "Jimmy, you'll be fine."

"I know."

"You be quick and then get back to your family."

"I will."

There were no long farewells. Just a nod from Carlisle's head and he disappeared into the darkness. If I'd known it was the last time that I'd see him face to face, maybe I would've said something profound.

CHAPTER ONE HUNDRED FIVE

I was emboldened now. Instead of walking, I took the tunnel at a trot. And it wasn't the guards that offered to take the lead; it was a couple of inmates.

"You're one of Carlisle's pigeons too," one of them said.

"Brave kid," the other said, a fat man with a gut that could stop a combine.

I preferred my first trip down the tunnel. This time we had flashlights, and though it made the going more accessible, this trip I could see the skittering of rats at the tunnel edges. Now the shaft felt like a living, breathing thing. A tube that seemed like it could suck us back in at any moment.

By the time we reached the other end, we were in a full run.

The lead prisoners took the door first, peering out and then sliding out sideways, the man with the belly grunted as his stomach brushed the steel door.

"Clear," came the quick whisper, and I was back outside.

"I'm never going in there again," the fat one said, sucking in a gutful of fresh air.

"Where are we going, kid?" asked Hicks.

I pointed in the right direction. "That way."

Hicks stepped off, gun in hand. "Let's go then."

I made like I was counting the men. In reality, I was waiting for the end of the train. I let the last man pass, a skinny guard who looked like he'd been in high school the week before. He gave a shy nod. The hand that held his gun trembled.

I let them get further ahead until they'd passed into the night. When they were gone, I went back the way we'd come. I sprinted this time, feeling in the bottom of my bones that Carlisle was in real peril.

CHAPTER ONE HUNDRED SIX

I breezed through the tunnel and back into the prison proper. The emergency generators blinked out the second I left the storage room. It left me bathed in black and silence.

Then the cacophony of fighting started up again. Rather than skirt my way around it, I aimed right for it. I snuck with my father's revolver in hand into the belly of the beast,. He'd inherited it from his father. My grandfather got it from his father.

I was the fourth in line. I'd fired it on a practice range before, and while I was no expert, I figured that in the long shot that I had to use it, I could at least keep it in hand. I held no illusions of shooting a moving target at fifty yards. But I could scare someone. At least that was the plan.

It was easier going now. Every door hung open. Someone had gone to great lengths to open the entire prison.

"*Fuckers!*" I heard someone scream, and then three shots in rapid succession—no more profanities from that guy after that.

I passed the body of a guard who'd once stood post on our front porch during a night drill. His nametag said Pemberly. I prayed for Guard Pemberly as I tried to ignore the neat hole in his forehead and the mottled spatter on the wall behind him.

In another room, I almost heaved when I saw a pile of four or five dead inmates; their limbs splayed like ragdolls.

All I had to do was follow the sound.

Follow the sound, Jimmy.

Carlisle had said that Dad was holding out, but holding out against whom?

The sound of boots beating pavement gave me just enough time to skitter to the shadows. Two guards and three inmates passed, all armed.

After waiting a few seconds, I took up the chase. It was easy to keep pace; they were hurrying even though not enough to let anyone catch them unawares. They trotted through the cellblock and then past the administrative offices. I recognized the clinic where we'd taken Larry.

I stopped to catch my breath and put a hand against the wall. My hand slipped on something slick. I peeled my hand away, and it was covered in blood.

I ran on to avoid puking on the spot.

CHAPTER ONE HUNDRED SEVEN

S moke greeted me at the exit. There was a succession of explosions that rattled the ground. I saw the guard/inmate detail sprint across the quad. I stayed put. No way I could make it across without being seen.

Think, Jimmy.

That's when the doubt seeped in. Who am I? I am a kid: a kid with a gun. I could get in big trouble. Worse, I could die. I could get shot or blown up.

Then I knew it. I remembered what I'd told Larry about being brave. I remembered something that Carlisle once said, "The difference between being brave and pretending to be brave—ain't no difference at all."

My knees knocked. I clamped my teeth together and gripped the revolver tighter.

Alright, then. I'll be the man I'm supposed to be.

I was lifting my foot off the deck when a voice behind me froze me to the spot.

"What the hell are you doing here?"

CHAPTER ONE HUNDRED EIGHT

"Denny," I breathed. The gun in hand sagged to my side.

"Jimmy," he said incredulously.

Something bothered me about him. He was as put together as ever. Not a smudge on his straight ironed shirt. He had an automatic rifle pointed at the floor. But it wasn't his clothes or his arsenal that concerned me. It was the way his eyes danced. Not with worry. Not with concern. They had a grotesque calm that made me want to run.

"You shouldn't be here," he repeated.

The gun at my side, my index finger curled around the trigger, as if by instinct.

"Where's my dad?" I said quietly.

That seemed to break Denny's trance. His eyes lit up like he realized who I was. "I was just going to help him."

"Where is he?"

Denny motioned with his head toward the source of gunfire. "He's in quite the jam. Not sure he'll make it out."

That's when it all came around. The pieces fit in with morbid perfection.

The gun in my hand shifted. "It was you."

CHAPTER ONE HUNDRED NINE

"What was me, Jimmy?" His weapon hadn't moved. "Everything."

He cocked his head. "Everything?"

Amazingly, he seemed to relax with every word while I tensed like an over-tuned piano.

"Where's Carlisle?"

Denny's eyes narrowed. Here was a different man. Gone was the Hollywood hero. This guy had the glint of crazy.

My gun came up.

He laughed and pointed at it. "Where'd you get that?"

"It's my dad's."

"Maybe you should've left it that way."

"It'll be mine one day."

A sly grin played at the corner of his mouth. "Might just be yours *today*."

There was a commotion and three forms burst into the room. Denny brought up his gun and took the first form in the chest, two shots in rapid succession. The inmate fell to the ground, dead to the world.

The second man took a round in the side of his face,

having tripped mid-fire. The man screamed and splashed face-first onto the ground. As a hand went up to search the wound, Denny put three more rounds into the poor guy's back.

Denny shifted to aim in on the third form, and I'm sure he had him in his sights, but he froze.

"Well," he said, a smile on his face, "look at what we've got here! Jimmy was just asking about you."

Carlisle looked from Denny to me and then back again.

"What are you doing with the boy, Boss Bell?"

"I should be asking you the same thing. It seems I've heard some interesting tales today about you and Jimmy here being best of friends. Now tell me that's not true, Carlisle. You can imagine what Warden Allen would think, may God soon rest his soul."

I was about to answer for Carlisle, but he cut me off with a glare.

"Nothing to it. Rumors, boss."

Denny shook his head. "Now, Carlisle, you and I both know that rumors tend to lead straight to the truth in our quaint little prison. So, tell me, what have you two been up to? Not getting a little hanky-panky in the greenhouse now, are you, Carlisle?"

"I saw you and Mrs. Bell," I blurted.

Denny's gaze turned to me, more curious than imposing.

"You saw us do what?"

The words spilled out like he'd ripped them from my brain. "Mrs. Bell was naked and dancing. You were sitting in a chair watching her. You slapped her butt, and she was crying."

It sounded juvenile coming out of my mouth.

Denny threw his head back and laughed. When he recovered, he said, "That's not against the law, Jimmy. Ask your best buddy here. Isn't that right, Carlisle? Not a damn thing wrong with a man admiring his wife."

"No, Boss."

"See, Jimmy? You happened to see some adult stuff that you're too young to understand. Just wait until you get a little older. Though I'm sure you won't be taking liberties with memories of my wife, now will you?"

I didn't fully comprehend what he was asking, yet I still shook my head.

"And as for you . . ." Denny turned to face Carlisle. The rifle came up. "I've had enough of your meddling."

I was across the room from the man, but that didn't mean a thing. I brought my dad's revolver up. My eyes looked over the sights. I pulled the trigger.

CHAPTER ONE HUNDRED TEN

Denny didn't jump or anything. He looked at me and then over his shoulder to where the bullet from the revolver had struck the wall. His head turned back, shaking.

"Seems like your daddy didn't teach you much about shooting. Take a kid like yourself. I'd say on a good day, you could've got me at seven, maybe ten yards. Look at me; I'm a good bit farther than that." He took four steps back to punctuate the point. The rifle shifted its aim from Carlisle to me. Denny tapped the barrel. "Now take this beauty. I could take you running at a hundred and fifty yards. If I'm sitting on a hill, I could hit you at five hundred. So, you see, I knew before you even took a shot that the cards stacked in my favor." The weapon went back to Carlisle. "Good try, boys. I'm not sure what you were trying to accomplish, but it looks like it's all in a day's—"

I pulled the trigger over and over until the hammer clicked home on an empty chamber, and there was nothing left but the beating boom of gunfire in my ears.

CHAPTER ONE HUNDRED ELEVEN

Well, two out of five ain't too shabby for a kid.

A pessimist would have said I'd missed with three of my five remaining shots. I'm no pessimist.

Denny was staring down at the two shots he'd taken in the chest. His jaw moved, but the only thing that came out was a wheezing whine like a pinched balloon.

The rifle clattered to the ground, and Denny followed shortly after.

Carlisle was on him in a flash, first kicking the rifle away and then checking the assistant warden for a pulse.

"He's dead."

The first thing I wanted to say was, "Good," but all I got out was some mumbled expletive. Denny had asked for it. He said Dad was dead or gonna be. Denny was going to kill Carlisle; I was sure of that. And while he might not have killed me, what would my life have been then?

I'm not sure how long Carlisle had been saying my name before I snapped back, my gun-toting-hand shaking.

"Jimmy?"

"I'm okay."

He slid the revolver from my hand and eased me to the ground. "Do you have any more ammunition?"

"In my backpack." My voice sounded cold and devoid of life. I was a robot, going through the required motions.

I felt the backpack lift from my shoulders and heard Carlisle rustling around inside while my eyes were glued to the open-mouthed corpse of Denny Bell. I didn't feel bad for killing him. I didn't even feel scared. I just . . . I didn't feel. I can't fully explain the sensation, even now, with the benefit of looking back from a distance.

Carlisle stepped into my field of vision and, before I could say anything, he emptied another six rounds into Denny's lifeless body.

My eyes widened at the surreal sight.

"You need to go, Jimmy," he said nervously. "Back the way you came. And this time, stay the hell home, you hear me?"

He'd shoved the revolver in his waistband and was helping me to my feet. There was no time for questions. I saw figures running our way.

"I can't leave you here; they'll—"

"Don't worry about me," he said, pushing me out the door. When we were at arm's length, he looked at me woefully. "You take care of yourself, Jimmy. Don't tell a soul about what happened here today."

"Okay." Tears welled in my eyes.

"Pinky swear?"

I nodded and held out my pinky. Carlisle took it with his.

"You remember everything I told you?"

"I will."

There were shouts from outside. They were about to come in.

"Now go."

Carlisle turned to meet the onslaught, arms raised, with what I now realize were hands covered in the residue expelled from Dad's revolver.

CHAPTER ONE HUNDRED TWELVE

That's it. That's the story of my becoming a murderer at age ten and some change.

There's more to it, however, and if you've stuck with me this far, maybe you'd like to hear it. I think you'll like it. It's about a boy and his dad.

First, the small details.

My old man survived. He and a handful of guards held off Denny Bell's guard and inmate mercenary gang. When they finally got inside the room, they naturally assumed Carlisle had killed the assistant warden. Dad said Carlisle admitted to it right away.

It wouldn't be until days later that Denny's involvement was entirely uncovered. The loose lips came from none other than Mrs. Bell herself. She told the local and federal authorities all about her dead husband's escapades. Not only was he a compulsive womanizer, but he'd also had a budding smuggling operation running through the prison for two years. With his brother on the prison board at the national level, Denny had assumed that he'd be the next pick for the warden.

But Dad had his own champions. Despite Denny running out the last warden, the Allen family still came to Virginia.

The entire operation had been planned to discredit my father and paint Denny in a favorable light. Once this came out, Denny's brother, a slick-mouthed attorney with proclivities similar to his younger brother, was arrested and charged with a rap sheet the size of a roll of paper towels.

As for Mrs. Bell, she never got to see the fruits of her admission. After telling the authorities everything she knew, she went home, kissed her children goodnight, and swallowed a half a gallon of Drano. I never understood why a person would choose such a method for self-murder. By all accounts, it was a messy and agonizing death.

For obvious reasons, my dad was transferred to another prison. Certain assurances were made that what had transpired was not the fault of the vaunted Warden Allen. But as things happen, everyone knew the score. Dad's reputation as The Fixer disappeared overnight. He never got a plum assignment again, but he continued to take his lumps for years. He would later retire with a healthy pension.

During that time, he and Mom split. I guess some adventures are too much for man and wife. Larry and I stayed with Mom, and we saw less and less of our father.

For years, I tried to find Carlisle. His case had gone underground because of the circumstances surrounding the final event. No one ever questioned me. I'd come out unscathed from the commotion, at least physically.

The mental game was another issue.

I couldn't snap out of my funk. The only thing I focused on was schoolwork, and that was for Carlisle and Kenji, of course. In the span of a few months, I'd lost my two best friends. How does anyone come back from that?

The short answer is, you don't. Not all the way.

By the time I was thirteen, I was sneaking drinks from

Mom's stash. By fifteen, I was running around with the worst kids in school.

I knew how to skirt the line. I never got arrested, but I always missed curfew. Sure, Mom would ground me for weeks. I railed and screamed, and she stood fast.

"I know you'll come back to me," she'd say. I laughed in her face.

I WAS eighteen when I found Carlisle. Some judge in some town found him guilty of killing Denny Bell. It turned out that once the wheels of justice got moving, there was little that could be done. Not that anyone tried, not even Carlisle. He took my punishment for me. It killed me to find that out. I was a murderer, and he was doing my time.

After several unsuccessful efforts to contact him, I fell into a deep depression. I found solace in a bottle a day that soon turned to two. I was a high school graduate with a year to live.

WHEN I TURNED NINETEEN, my father invited me to his cabin in the Smokies. I agreed because I knew he kept the place stocked with booze to the gills. Lucky me.

The first day, I was good. Just a couple of drinks. The second day, I snuck shots. Third day, I blacked out.

I woke to find Dad sitting in a chair at the small desk he sometimes used to write letters to old friends. He still clung to the old ways despite the rise of the Internet age.

"How do you feel?" he asked.

"Like shit."

He nodded, tapped his shirt pocket for the cigarettes that

were no longer there. He'd quit at some point. I'm not sure when. He never stopped tapping his pocket.

"I think you should see someone."

This idea was rich. Here was the man who'd dragged us around for years, the man who'd made Mom miserable. Turns out that a man who's married to his work can't be married to his wife. He was the man who was responsible for the wreck I'd become. And he wanted me to see someone?

"No way." I stripped the blanket covering me and almost fell to the side when the headache spiked me.

"Not so fast. I made some calls."

Great. Dad wanted me to go to rehab. Or was it counseling? Neither option tickled my funny bone. AA was for quitters. I used to say that as a toast.

"Thanks for the good time, Dad. Let me shower, and I'll be out of your hair for good."

I meant every word; I was done with him. I was done with everyone. Hell, I was done with myself. The guilt I felt left a hole in me as wide as the Grand Canyon.

"It's Carlisle," he said.

I turned so fast that my head spun. I had to reach out and grab the headboard to steady myself.

"What did you say?"

"I said it's Carlisle."

"What about him?" I asked through teeth that could tear apart a jaguar.

"I think you should see him. Talk to him. Whatever you want."

The anger deflated like I'd been popped.

"When?"

"Whenever you're ready."

CHAPTER ONE HUNDRED THIRTEEN

We went to see Carlisle two days later. I told Dad I wanted to go in alone, and he allowed it. I had aged a millennium, but Carlisle still looked as young and carefree as I remembered. He smiled that wide grin when I sat down on the other side of the plexiglass. We both picked up one side of the phones.

"Jimmy."

My words came out in a spill. "How are you, Carlisle?" I had so much to say and none of the words to say them. "I'm so sorry. If you want me to—"

He raised a hand.

"It's good to see you, Jimmy. Let's start there. I've missed you."

I remember feeling such anger at his blasé attitude. I'd come in sporting a good buzz, and he was ruining it.

"How can you say that? After what happened? I'm a terrible person. You should—"

His steady gaze speared me to silence like he'd clamped my jaw shut with a vise. "I'm ready to tell you my story."

It took me back years, to his promise in that wonderful greenhouse in Virginia.

"Your story?"

He nodded.

"I swallowed my first pill at fifteen. I did it to fit in. From there . . ."

CHAPTER ONE HUNDRED FOURTEEN

That was the first of many visits. Sometimes I talked, and Carlisle listened. Other times I sat and tried to fix my mind on what he was saying. It felt good to be with my friend again.

Gradually, after many subsequent trips over state lines, we got around to the subject of my life. He'd told me his story, and now I told him mine. I told him about my guilt, the running around, and finally the drinking. Carlisle never judged me. In fact, the only thing he said was, "When you're ready to fix that, you know where I live."

It took many months, countless meetings, and hours spent with Carlisle, but I did it. I got sober despite the relapses and the near-crippling guilt. It was always right there in front of me when I saw Carlisle. Through it all, he never offered advice. He would tell me some tidbit of his own experience, and I sat in wonder at his sage-like wisdom. He gave me my strength and hope.

"Will I have to do this for the rest of my life?" I asked one day.

"If you want to stay alive."

At that moment, I did. I did want to live. The visits with Carlisle meant more to me than anything, and yet, the rest of my life was incrementally getting better.

"Progress, not perfection," Carlisle said, over and over.

I celebrated one year of sobriety by telling Carlisle that I was going back to school.

"Business?" he asked. He liked to talk about getting out and opening a burger stand somewhere, maybe at the beach.

"Law school," I said with a proud smile.

Carlisle whistled into the phone. "You working for our side or theirs?"

I laughed. "Haven't decided yet, but probably yours."

"Will I have to call you Mr. Bigshot after you graduate?" I fixed him with a stare.

"I'm going to get you out, Carlisle. I promise."

IT TOOK years and much-needed help from my father, but we finally got the prison board to approve Carlisle's parole. Up until that point, he had close to forty years behind bars.

It didn't hurt that he'd helped many inmates get sober, and he'd been instrumental with other prisons instituting programs to help battle a variety of addictions.

The day I told Carlisle about his upcoming release was his birthday. I had a huge cookie made with "Happy Birthday! We did it!" slathered in cream cheese frosting on top.

I was his attorney, but still we couldn't hug. Rules are rules.

I should've broken them.

Anyway, now on to the good part.

EPILOGUE

My wife and two kids are with me. My youngest, Carlisle, has my left leg in a death grip.

"When can we go home?" he asks.

"After we meet Daddy's friend," my wife Cora says.

I'm too choked up to talk. Lucky for Cora. And for the call with Larry on the way. My brother's headmaster at a boarding school that looks like Hogwarts. Cora and Larry's combined optimism is the only reason I'm standing right now.

We hear a loud screech as the oil-lacking door to the prison opens. I remember my vow to carry WD-40 as part of my spy tool kit. A guard steps out and I exhale. It's not Carlisle.

Then another form, tall and proud, emerges behind the first. He was grayer now but no less proud.

"Is that him?" my oldest son asks.

"That's him," I say, unable to keep the emotion from my voice.

Cora squeezes my hand and then lets it go.

"Go see him," she says.

I nod my thanks, tears spilling from my eyes, down my cheeks, and onto my son's head.

I step away from my family, hesitant at first like he might reject me now that he's out. But that's silly, *this* is Carlisle. He is my friend. He is my brother.

His eyes meet mine. There's a look on his face like an angel who's just been given his wings. It's true. This is indeed what has happened.

The guard says something to him that I can't hear. Carlisle nods and shakes the man's hand, and now walks towards me.

My body is trying to process the fear, hope, glee, and pure adrenaline. My legs are shaking. I'm weeping openly.

We stop when we're two strides apart. He looks at me and I at him.

"Jimmy," he says.

"Carlisle."

We stand there for a long moment.

When he steps forward, I break the rules.

I've stumbled across the finish line. I've let go of the past and forgiven myself in whole.

But most importantly, and no matter what happens next, my prayers have been answered. Another son has come home.

I hope you enjoyed this story.
If you did, please take a moment to write a review <u>on Amazon.</u> Even the short ones help!

Want to stay in the loop?
Sign Up at cg-cooper.com to be the FIRST to learn about new releases.
Plus get newsletter only bonus content for FREE.

A portion of all profits from the sale of my novels goes to fund OPERATION C4, our nonprofit initiative serving young military officers. For more information visit OperationC4.com.

ALSO BY C. G. COOPER

Broken

Tested

The Tom Greer Novels

A Life Worth Taking

Stand Alone Novels

To Live

The Warden's Son

The Interrogators

Higgins

The Spy In Residence Novels

What Lies Hidden

The Alex Knight Novels

Breakout

The Stars & Spies Series:

Backdrop

The Patriot Protocol Series:

The Patriot Protocol

The Chronicles of Benjamin Dragon:

Benjamin Dragon – Awakening

Benjamin Dragon – Legacy

Benjamin Dragon - Genesis

ABOUT THE AUTHOR

C. G. Cooper is the *USA TODAY* and AMAZON BESTSELLING author of the CORPS JUSTICE novels (including spinoffs), The Chronicles of Benjamin Dragon and various other novels.

Cooper grew up in a Navy family and traveled from one Naval base to another as he fed his love of books and a fledgling desire to write.

Upon graduating from the University of Virginia with a degree in Foreign Affairs, Cooper was commissioned in the United States Marine Corps and went on to serve six years as an infantry officer. C. G. Cooper's final Marine duty station was in Nashville, Tennessee, where he fell in love with the laid-back lifestyle of Music City.

His first published novel, BACK TO WAR, came out of a need to link back to his time in the Marine Corps. That novel, written as a side project, spawned many follow-on novels, several exciting spinoffs, and catapulted Cooper's career.

Cooper lives just south of Nashville with his wife, three children, and their German shorthaired pointer, Liberty, who's become a popular character in the Corps Justice novels.

When he's not writing, Cooper spends time with his family, does his best to improve his golf handicap, and loves to shed light on the ongoing fight of everyday heroes.

Cooper loves hearing from readers and responds to every email personally.
To connect with C. G. Cooper visit
www.cg-cooper.com

Made in the USA
Monee, IL
09 December 2019

18209504R00192